The fizzy, bright feeling was back.

And getting stronger. He kept on looking at her. Admiringly. Almost hopefully. She stared at his mouth and wondered what his lips would feel like touching hers. She thought about how she really would like, someday, to find out.

And then the phone rang.

Dax didn't answer it. And for a moment there, he'd almost thought that Zoe was about to make a move on him. And being human and male, he'd wanted her to. A lot.

Which made him pretty damn stupid, right? If the phone hadn't rung, if she had made a move on him, he would very likely have taken her up on it.

And then, one way or another, he'd have wound up losing the best assistant he'd ever had.

He wasn't sure if he was relieved. Or furious.

Dear Reader,

Zoe Bravo is beyond tired of being called the "free spirit" of the family. She wants a job that holds her interest and she wants to gain her family's respect.

Working as billionaire bachelor Dax Girard's assistant seems perfect. Constant variety, travel to exotic locations and a chance to get a start in magazine publishing. What's not to love?

Well, the boss first of all—yes, he's dreamy and all the women are after him. But when it comes to his assistant, he wants to keep things strictly professional. That's fine with Zoe. The last thing she's after is a hot date with Dax. If only she could convince everyone else in the office that there is no way she'll be like all his other assistants. She will not be falling for the boss.

But then again, Dax is a very exciting man. And when he looks at her with those bedroom eyes of his, well, sometimes it's hard to remember that it's the job that matters. Sometimes it's hard not to yearn for one long, tender kiss. Sometimes it's hard not to wonder if Dax might be trying to tempt her into breaking the rules *he* made in the first place....

Happy reading everyone,

Christine Rimmer

EXPECTING THE BOSS'S BABY

CHRISTINE RIMMER

SPECIAL EDITION®

Published by Silhouette Books

America's Publisher of Contemporary Romance

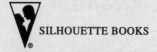 **SILHOUETTE BOOKS**

ISBN-13: 978-0-373-65559-5

Recycling programs
for this product may
not exist in your area.

EXPECTING THE BOSS'S BABY

Copyright © 2010 by Christine Rimmer

Visit Silhouette Books at www.eHarlequin.com

Printed in U.S.A.

CHRISTINE RIMMER

came to her profession the long way around. Before settling down to write about the magic of romance, she'd been everything from an actress to a salesclerk to a waitress. Now that she's finally found work that suits her perfectly, she insists she never had a problem keeping a job—she was merely gaining "life experience" for her future as a novelist. Christine is grateful not only for the joy she finds in writing, but for what waits when the day's work is through: a man she loves, who loves her right back, and the privilege of watching their children grow and change day to day. She lives with her family in Oklahoma. Visit Christine at www.christinerimmer.com.

For you, the reader.
May your holiday season be filled with love and light
and the joy of family togetherness.

Chapter One

"Can I lay it right out for you?" Dax Girard asked.

Sitting across his wide black desk from him, Zoe Bravo answered earnestly, "Yes, of course. Please do." She did want this job. She wanted it bad. She had things to prove—to herself and to her family.

He arched a straight dark eyebrow. "You're really pretty."

Oh, please. Was he going to hit on her? Right here, during the interview? Euuu.

He wasn't finished. "And if I were to meet you under other circumstances, I would be only too happy to have sex with you. But I need good staff, above all. So I have a house rule. You work for me, that's *all* you do with me."

Zoe stifled a burst of inappropriate laugher and sat up straighter in the chair. Somehow, she managed to reply with a straight face, "Seriously, it's not a problem. I've known you for what, two minutes?"

Had that sounded sarcastic? Maybe a little.

But he *had* just told her he wouldn't sleep with her—when she hadn't even asked him to. He deserved a dose of attitude.

If he noticed the edge to her tone, he let it pass. "I think your mother is a wonderful woman."

"She certainly is." Zoe's mom, Aleta Randall Bravo, was from an old San Antonio family. Aleta knew *everyone,* including the great adventurer and magazine publisher Dax Girard. It was her mom who had recommended her to Dax for this job, which meant Dax would most likely want to give Zoe a chance. People generally tried to please her mom. And not only because of the social connection thing either. There was something about Aleta that made you like her—and want *her* to like *you.*

He said, "And you seem…bright. I have a good feeling about you. I want to make this work."

"Great," Zoe answered, trying to sound positive and upbeat. "I do, too."

"But I just need to have this clear with you, straight from the gate. Sex is absolutely off the table."

She didn't groan—but she really, really wanted to. Enough about sex already. How many times did she have to promise not to put a move on him?

Okay, yeah. He was hot—in that rich-guy, lean, preppy way. He looked like he played a lot of tennis. He probably jogged with his shirt off and gave all the women he wasn't going to have sex with a thrill.

And she'd heard the stories about him, about how women found him irresistible. But not Zoe. She wanted a job, not a hot date. "I promise you, Dax. I'll manage to control myself. Somehow."

A long pause ensued. Zoe tried to look calm and competent and unconcerned while he stared at her steadily, his sexy, deep brown eyes narrowed. Probing. Apparently, he found it impossible to believe that she wouldn't try and jump his bones at the earliest opportunity.

But then, at last, he dipped his handsome head of thick, wavy sable hair to study her résumé again. "Let's see here. You were on the campus papers at two colleges. You type ninety words a minute, you know Microsoft Office."

"Backward and forward, yes."

"You've been to UT, Stanford and Brandeis, I see, majoring in Journalism and English."

"So I know how magazine publishing works. Also, my spelling and punctuation skills are solid. I know my grammar." What else could she say? Not too much about college. Yes, she'd attended the best schools. Too bad she'd never actually graduated from any of them. She *was* bright and she learned fast. But she'd always been... easily distracted, eager for the next life experience. And impatient with mundane activities like regularly attending classes and plodding through her assignments. She threw in, "I thrive in a fast-paced environment and I'm very much at home with multitasking."

"All good." He glanced up at her. "I understand you're also an excellent amateur photographer, right?" His gaze was probing again. Was this a trick question?

She met his eyes levelly. "I enjoy photography, yes. It's a hobby of mine."

"I believe I saw some of your work at the Texas State Endowment Ball and Auction last month, didn't I?"

"I suppose you did. I shot the pictures and the short film presentation for the chopper you won." He'd bid six figures on the custom motorcycle, which had made the Texas State Endowment people, including Zoe's mother, who chaired the event, very happy.

Dax smiled then. It was a stunningly gorgeous smile that created manly crinkles at the corners of his fine, dark eyes. "I love that bike. Your brother is a genius."

"Yes, he is." Jericho, sixth-born of the nine children in her family, designed and built custom motorcycles. He'd donated the chopper for the auction.

Dax was looking severe again. "*Great Escapes* is a travel magazine. And we do hire photographers. It's even possible that eventually some of your work might be used in a story...." He let the sentence trail off.

She gave him a cool smile. "I thought we were discussing a job as your assistant."

"You're right. We are. And that's why it's important that we understand each other."

So then they had a problem. A big one. She didn't understand this guy at all.

He was still talking. "You would have your hands full fielding my calls, dealing with catering for meetings, handling my correspondence and any other of a thousand and one tasks I'll be assigning to you. It's doubtful you'd be getting your big break as a photographer."

Zoe had to be honest with herself. This was not looking very promising. In spite of how much he admired her mother, he'd decided not to hire her. And by now, she was less than sure she wanted this job anyway. She crossed her legs, smoothed her slim skirt over her knees and said drily, "No sex, no pictures. Got it."

He slanted her a look of purely male appreciation— and wasn't there a hint of humor in that dark glance, as well? "Sorry." All at once he looked kind of boyish and awkward. That surprised her. Until then, she'd never thought of Dax Girard as anything but all grown-up, a little too sophisticated—and way too concerned about not having sex with her. "I'm trying to cover all the bases here," he said. "The truth is I haven't had such great luck choosing my assistants in the past."

Judging by the way he'd managed this interview, she wasn't surprised.

He added, "Twice, I tried just letting HR handle it." His mouth formed a grim line. "That didn't work out either."

It was none of her business, but she asked anyway. "Why not?"

He looked slightly pained. "I want someone efficient and professional. But not scary. Not…intimidating. I like a *little* personality in my assistant. Someone easy on the eyes. And a sense of humor is a must. HR couldn't seem to strike the right balance on that."

She realized that all his talk of sex and photography had not only annoyed her and made her wonder if she really wanted this job after all, but it had also somehow served to ease her nervousness. She spoke frankly, "I don't know what else to tell you, Dax. I do have a personality. A pretty strong one, to be honest. I want an interesting job that doesn't require the college degree I don't have. Working for you just might be perfect. I subscribe to your magazine. I like the layout. The articles are fun and informative and make me want to visit the places I'm reading about. And I enjoy your editorials. And being your assistant would probably offer me a lot of variety, of varying kinds of responsibilities, which means I wouldn't be bored."

He stared out toward the big windows that provided

a prime view of San Antonio real estate. "Well, yes. Variety, you'll get. Beyond the usual, you'll have some minor editorial responsibilities, probably assist on things like the calendar shoot." The *Great Escapes* calendar featured gorgeous women wearing skimpy clothing in a wide range of beautiful settings. "You would have to expect to travel—not in the first few months, but certainly after I have time to learn to count on you."

She brightened at the thought. "The monthly Spotlight?" Seven or eight months a year, when he didn't use a contributing editor for the Spotlight, Dax personally traveled to some exotic locale for his feature story.

"Yes," he said. "The Spotlight."

She told him candidly, "I'm not looking for an office romance or a chance to break out my Nikon and start shooting. Just a job, Dax. Just *this* job."

He frowned some more. And then he stood up. "All right. Let's give it a try."

She couldn't believe it. He was hiring her after all. She bounced to her feet and took his offered hand.

He said, "There's a two-week trial period, starting Monday. At the end of the two weeks, we talk again. We evaluate and make a decision on whether or not you stay on. Welcome to *Great Escapes*."

She smiled then, a wide smile. If she liked working here, she would definitely be staying on—because she intended to make herself irreplaceable. "Thank you, Dax."

"Monday. Check in with HR at eight-thirty."

"I will. See you then."

Dax sank back into his chair and watched Zoe Bravo go. She had a great walk, smooth, with just a hint of a sway to her softly curving hips. He liked her smile and those beautiful blue eyes.

But would she make a good assistant?

He had no clue. As he'd openly confessed to her, hiring editorial assistants was not his strong suit. In fact, he was lousy at it.

But he had liked her instantly, had wished he could ask her out instead of giving her a job. However, he'd felt a certain obligation to carry through with the offer he had made to her mother. Aleta Bravo was a charming woman. And he was pleased to be able to help her daughter get a start in publishing.

At the very least, he had a feeling Aleta's daughter would be amusing. She would keep things lively around the office. He liked things lively.

And miracles did happen, didn't they, now and then? Zoe just might turn out to be efficient, organized and hardworking, to have a talent for the magazine business.

Then he would get over his attraction to her and be grateful to have found her.

If not, well, it wasn't as though he'd made a lifetime commitment to her. For once, he'd had the good sense to give himself an easy out. After fourteen days, he could simply let her go.

And he would. If she wasn't a good fit, he would fire her two weeks from Monday with no hesitation.

And then he would ask her to have dinner with him.

Zoe's cell started ringing when she got off the elevator on the ground floor: her mother. She smiled at the cute guy behind the security desk and tucked the BlackBerry back in her purse without answering it.

But then it rang again as she got in her car. Her mom must be wondering—and getting impatient about it.

"Hey, Mom."

"Well?"

"He hired me."

"Oh, I knew it. I think you'll love this job, sweetheart."

"I think so, too." Or at least, she would if her new boss would only realize that the job was *all* she was after. "But I'm not locked in yet. It's a two-week trial and then we'll discuss a permanent position."

"A trial? Is that usual?"

Zoe almost let herself get defensive. But not quite. It was a reasonable question after all. "I gather he hasn't had good luck with his assistants. He's a little trigger-shy. But that's okay. I am going to be terrific."

"I know you are." Her mom was smiling. Zoe could hear it in her voice.

"Thanks for the heads-up on this, Mom."

"I want to help. You know that."

"I do know." She stuck her key in the ignition. "Okay, then. I'm on my way to the salon next." She blew a long strand of chestnut hair out of her eyes. "I seriously need a cut. Gotta look good for my first day on the job. Love you and see you soon."

"Wait."

"Hmm?"

"We haven't seen you for Sunday dinner at the ranch in a while...."

Zoe made a grim face at herself as she adjusted the rearview mirror. Bravo Ridge, the family ranch, was a short drive from San Antonio. Zoe's mom and dad lived in SA, but most weekends they went to the ranch. Sunday dinner was kind of a family tradition. Not all the

Bravo siblings made it every time, but they each made an effort to show up at least every month or two.

Zoe hadn't gone in a while, not since early spring. She knew she was past due to put in an appearance.

"Zoe, honey, you still there?"

"Right here, Mom."

"Say you'll come."

Zoe imagined her dad, Davis, getting all up in her face, calling her his little free spirit, teasing her in that totally annoying way he had, wondering aloud how long *this* job would last. "I don't know, Mom. I have so much I need to do this weekend."

"Please, honey. It really has been way too long." Like most mothers, Aleta knew when to whip out the guilt card.

Zoe turned the key. Her cute little BMW's precision engine purred to life. "All right. I'll be there."

"Great." The pleasure in her mom's voice was almost worth the potential headache of dealing with her dad. "Dinner's at three or so, but come anytime."

Sunday, she got to the ranch at quarter of three just as everyone was sitting down in the dining room.

Her dad was aggravatingly hearty. "Zoe. How's my little girl?"

"Great, Dad. Doing well." She put on a big smile and reminded herself that when he said "little girl," he meant it with love. And she *was* his youngest child— well, if you didn't count Elena, her half sister, who was a year younger. She went to him and he grabbed her in a hug.

When she tried to slip free, he put his big hands on her shoulders and held her in place. "What in the hell did you do to your hair?"

I am not going to let him get to me. She eased free of his grip and smoothed the thick curls that fell below her shoulders. "I always wanted to be a redhead. Now I am." Like most of her decisions, she'd made it on the fly Thursday, after her interview with Dax Girard, when she went in for a cut. She'd stared at her reflection in her hairdresser's mirror and decided she was beyond tired of having brown hair. It had to go.

And no matter what her father said, she knew the vibrant red looked good on her. It set off her fair skin and blue eyes.

"Ahem, well," said her dad. "It's very—"

"You look so hot." Marnie, her brother Jericho's bride of a little over a month now, came to her rescue.

Zoe turned gratefully into new sister-in-law's embrace. "Hey. How's married life?"

Marnie released her and slanted a happy glance toward her groom. Jericho slowly smiled. It was hard to believe he'd always been the family's troubled loner. He didn't seem the least troubled now. For the first time, he was really happy. With his life. And his new wife.

"It's good," said Marnie. "It's very, very good."

"You look beautiful, honey," Aleta declared, already in her chair. Zoe went over and kissed her mom's cheek and then sat down.

They began passing the platters of juicy T-bones, corn on the cob and baked potatoes.

It was a big turnout for a family Sunday. Everyone had shown up this time except for Travis, youngest of the boys. Travis was always off on some oil rig somewhere.

Matt and Corrine's six-year-old, Kira, told them all about her new puppy, Rosie. "Rosie loves Kathleen," she announced. Kathleen was Matt and Corrine's second child, born the previous September. "Rosie wants to lick Kathleen all over. That's what a dog does when she wants to give you a kiss. She licks you. It's kind of icky and they slobber, you know? But Mommy says it's only from love, so it's all right."

It was nice, Zoe thought, to have a few little kids around now for family gatherings. Her brother Luke and his wife, Mercy, had a boy, Lucas. Gabe's wife, Mary, had a girl from her first marriage; Ginny was two now. Gabe doted on her. And Tessa, Ash's wife and Marnie's older sister, was four and a half months pregnant, so another niece or nephew was on the way.

After the meal, Zoe played pool in the game room, doubles, Marnie and Jericho versus Zoe and Abilene, who was Zoe's older sister by a year. As she bent over the table to set up a bank shot, Zoe realized she was having a great time. Really, she had to remember how much she enjoyed her family. She needed to show up at these things more often, not let her dad's careless remarks keep her away.

Around seven, she thanked Luke, who lived at the ranch full-time. She hugged Jericho and Marnie and headed for the door.

Her dad caught her as she was making her escape. "Zoe, hold on." She felt the knot of tension gather at the back of her neck as he strode toward her. He was sixty now, but he still carried himself as if he owned the world—and everyone in it.

She braced herself for more criticism. But he only grabbed her in a last hug and told her not to be a stranger.

She looked at up at him and smiled. "I won't, Dad. I love you."

Gruffly, he gave the words back to her. "And I love you, too. Very much."

Her car waited in the circular drive at the foot of the wide front steps. She slid in behind the wheel, turned the engine on and rolled down the windows. The hot June wind blew in and ruffled her newly red hair. For a moment, she just sat there, staring at the ranch house, which was big and white and modeled after the governor's mansion, complete with giant Doric columns marching impressively along the wide front verandah.

Then she laughed and gunned the engine and took off around the circle and down the long front driveway, headed back to SA and her own cute, cozy condo. Life, right then, seemed very good, indeed. She was young and strong and ready, at last, to be more focused, more mature, less…easily distracted.

Her new job at *Great Escapes* magazine began tomorrow. She couldn't wait to get started.

"What in the hell did you do to your hair?"

Those were Dax's first words to her Monday morning, when he got off the elevator and saw her sitting at her new desk where the HR person had left her.

Zoe pressed her lips together to stifle a cutting reply. She really didn't want to start right off trading insults with the boss.

But on the other hand, she needed to be herself or this job wouldn't last any longer than any of the others had. Being herself would have to include fighting back when Dax pissed her off.

And anyway, hadn't he said he wanted someone with personality?

She yanked open the pencil drawer, grabbed the

dagger-shaped letter opener from the tray within, raised it high and stabbed the air with it. "Do you realize that is exactly what my father said to me yesterday at Sunday dinner?"

He moved back a step and eyed the letter opener sideways.

She pressed her point—both literally and figuratively. "You don't need to know all the issues I've got with my dad. You just need to know there *are* issues and you would do well not to turn out to be too much like him."

With gratifying caution, Dax inquired, "Are you really planning to stab me with that thing?"

"Oh, I guess not." She dropped it back in the pencil tray and shoved the drawer shut again. "I have to face facts. If I kill you, who will sign my paychecks?"

He was still staring at her hair. "Okay. Now that I'm over the shock, I admit it suits you," he grumbled.

She gave him her sweetest smile. "I'll take that as a compliment. And we can move on."

"Coffee first," he commanded low.

She peered at him more closely. Killer handsome, of course. But tired, too. There were dark circles under those wonderful bedroom eyes. "Long night?"

"Aren't they all?" He named a place around the corner where the lattes were excellent. "Petty cash in the bottom drawer."

She pulled out the drawer in question. There was a little safe mounted inside, with a combination lock. He rattled off the combination. She grabbed a pencil and jotted the numbers on a sticky note.

He said, "Get me the strongest coffee they've got, black, extra-large. When you bring it in to me, come armed with a notebook or your laptop and we'll get down to what I want from you today. After that, you get with Lin Dietrich." He turned and gazed over the large open workspace of desks, tables, machines and semi-cubicles. "Lin!"

A slim, beautiful Asian woman with a streak of cobalt blue in her thick, straight black bangs popped up from behind a glass partition. "What now?"

Dax signaled her over. When she reached his side, he announced proudly, "Lin's the best editorial assistant I ever had, which means I had to promote her. My loss. Your gain. Lin is features editor now. But today, she'll be with you, showing you everything you need to know."

Lin gave Dax a narrow look, and then sent a wry smile in Zoe's direction. "Because there's nothing I need more than a little extra work to do."

"I learn fast," Zoe promised.

"Best news I've heard so far today." Lin's expression said she'd believe it when she saw it.

"Coffee," Dax said one more time, in a pained voice. He turned and went into his office without waiting for a reply, swinging the door firmly shut behind him.

Lin laughed. "He's always at his most charming on Monday mornings. Better get that coffee. I'm here when you're ready for me."

Dax finished telling Zoe what he wanted from her at a little after ten. She found Lin, who took a few minutes to introduce her around the office. More than one of her new colleagues teased her about falling for the boss. Wearily, Zoe reassured each one that it wasn't going to be a problem.

Once the introductions were made, Lin then began

guiding her through the mile-long list of high-priority duties Dax had given her.

At noon, she and Lin went to a coffee shop down the street for a quick lunch.

"I feel it's only right that I say something," Lin warned. "I can't stress it strongly enough. If you fall for him, he will have to let you go."

Zoe made the sign of the cross. "Lin. Please. Not you, too."

"Did Dax warn you about the problem?"

"Repeatedly. And you heard the others back at the office. The subject is getting seriously old."

"I'm sorry, but it's an issue. You don't have to take my word for it. Just wait. You'll see. He loves women. Women love him. They can't seem to help it. He can't seem to say no."

Zoe sipped her iced tea. "What about you? You were his assistant once. Did *you* fall in love with him?"

"Uh-uh. I had my secret weapon." Lin held up her left hand. She wore a thick platinum wedding band.

"A husband."

Lin beamed. "Roger." She sighed in a dreamy way. "He's an aerospace engineer." She pulled her wallet from her giant black tote and took out a picture. Roger had blond hair, an angular face and thick-rimmed black glasses. "Hot, huh?"

"Very handsome."

"He's the only man for me." Lin pressed the picture to her heart before tucking it away in her wallet again. "So I'm immune."

"But what about every other woman in the office? I haven't heard any predictions that *they're* doomed to fall for Dax. What makes me so special?"

Lin shrugged. "It's the constant proximity, I think.

The daily close exposure to him when you work directly for him. I don't know what it is about him. He must have some genetic anomaly. An excess of sex pheromones maybe."

"Oh, come on. You're not serious."

"Oh, but I am." Lin tipped her head, studying Zoe. "And you're exactly his type." The blue streak in her hair caught the light, gleaming. "It's sad, really. I tend to think of it as Dax's fatal flaw. He hires the pretty ones with personality. And then they fall head-over-heels for him."

"Not me. Can we be done talking about this?"

Lin picked up her fork and stuck it in her Cobb salad. "Too bad you're not already in love with someone else."

…in love with someone else….

The words bounced around in Zoe's brain.

Lin was right. Zoe needed a man. *Her* man. A man she adored, who adored her in return. Such a man would be the perfect way to get everyone at *Great Escapes* to stop predicting her inevitable, job-destroying, hopeless passion for the boss.

Too bad her man didn't exist—or if he did, Zoe had failed, so far, to meet him.

She pushed her coleslaw around on her plate, considering. Not that she was in any way ready for her own personal hero, not yet. She had things to prove, a success to make in the business world, before she found the man for her and settled down.

Besides, right now she didn't need an actual guy. No way. She didn't have the time for a flesh-and-blood Mr. Wonderful who would drag along love and commitment and a shared mortgage. Uh-uh. It was the idea of the guy that mattered. It was that everyone *believed* she had a guy who was the only guy for her.

She slanted Lin a glance. "Maybe I *am* in love already."

Sharp black eyes widening, Lin looked up from her plate. "There *is* someone special, then?"

"I...don't want to say anything right now. It's, um, well, it's complicated."

"Complicated is fine. Whatever. As long as there's someone and you're in love with him."

"You really think so?"

"I know so. If you're serious about getting a start at *Great Escapes,* a special guy would be the best thing for you. And for Dax. *And* for the poor, overworked ladies down in HR."

Chapter Two

Zoe took that whole week to make up her mind.

Really, it was a wild idea. Not to mention a total lie. She didn't want to get involved in an elaborate fiction if she could avoid it. It could be dangerous. There was always the possibility she would get caught, and not only by tripping herself up. What if Dax ran into her mother or father or someone in the family and happened to mention that Zoe had a fiancé?

That could be embarrassing.

But, then, as far as tripping up, she could make notes, create her own personal hero from the ground up, so that he became the next thing to real for her. Then she would be unlikely to contradict herself when she spoke of him.

And as far as her family, well, how much chance was there that they would blow the whistle on her? It wasn't as though Dax knew her family well, or hung around with them or anything. Even if he ran into her mother somewhere, it would only be *Hello, how are you? And have a nice day.*

True, her mom might ask how Zoe was doing on the job. He would say how great she was—well, he'd *better* say how great she was, because she intended to be even better at the job than Lin had been—and that would be that.

No reason a fiancé even had to come up.

And she wouldn't have to tell the lie forever. Eventually, when she was certain that Dax had stopped worrying she might try to seduce him, when everyone in the office quit waiting for her to drag him into the supply closet and ravish him, she could end it with her imaginary groom-to-be. Because, well, sadly, sometimes even the most perfect relationships don't last.

Yeah. It was workable. Totally workable.

Still, she hesitated. Maybe if she just held tight, the issue would resolve itself. Dax and everyone else at the office would see she wasn't the least interested in him and that would be that.

She wished.

Unfortunately, as that first week went by, it was becoming painfully clear that the issue was not resolving itself, that she *had* to do something.

Because Dax really was very attractive. He was so smart and funny. So yummy to look at. And he always smelled wonderful—fresh and clean, a little minty. And way too manly.

And now and then, she'd catch him watching her in a speculative way. As though he was attracted to her, too. As if he saw the inevitable approaching and wasn't dreading it all that much, that she was bound to make a pass at him and he was bound to take her up on it.

And then he would have to tell her that she wasn't working out. She'd be out of a job and her father would give her a hard time about it, once more making Sunday dinner at the ranch an experience she only wanted to avoid.

Thursday, as she was trying to make some headway organizing Dax's bottomless pile of slush submissions, the elevator doors rolled wide and a tall brunette in four-inch cage heels and satin cargoes stepped off. She smoothed her Grecian-style chiffon top, which had a plunging neckline that lovingly revealed a lot of ripe, tanned cleavage.

"Dax, please." She ordered him up like a cocktail, in a husky voice, batting her big Bambi eyes.

"Have a seat. I'll just buzz him and see if he's—"

"Oh, he'll see me." The woman breezed right on by.

"Wait. You can't…"

But apparently, she could. She already had his door open and was lounging seductively against the door frame. "Dax."

"Faye," he said from within. "What a surprise."

Zoe jumped up. "Uh, Faye, if you'll only wait a minute, I'll just—"

Dax cut her off. "It's all right, Zoe." Did he sound annoyed—with her, for not stopping the woman in time? Or with Faye, for popping up out of nowhere to lounge against his office door? Zoe couldn't tell. And she couldn't read his expression, as Faye was blocking her view. "Hold my calls," he instructed.

"Uh. Sure."

Faye sent a triumphant smile over her shoulder as she went in and shoved the door shut with the tall heel of her cage shoe.

When she came out twenty-eight minutes later, there was no mistaking the glow to her cheeks and the swollen, red, very-much-kissed look about her full lips. The dark brown hair was a bit mussed. And the Grecian-inspired top draped a little differently than when she'd gone in.

She blew a tender kiss in through the open doorway. "Tomorrow night?"

"I can't wait," came Dax's deep, smooth voice from inside the office.

With one last knowing glance in Zoe's general direction, Faye strutted into the elevator. The doors slowly closed. Zoe shifted her gaze back to her computer screen. She stared blindly at a proposal titled, "Pack It Lite: Never Check a Bag Again," and tried to figure out exactly what she was feeling.

It couldn't be jealousy, could it?

It couldn't be that she could actually picture *herself* coming out of Dax's office with her shirt on crooked and her hair all wild?

No. Absolutely not. She wanted this job. She *liked* this job. And nothing—especially not a burning desire to get down with the boss—was going to mess this up for her.

Friday, when she came in after lunch, Dax called her in for an afternoon huddle.

They had a lot to do and a short time to do it in. He would be gone from the office after next Wednesday. Thursday morning, he and a photographer and Lulu Grimes, one of the associate editors, were off to Melbourne for the December Spotlight, "Aussie Holiday."

He would be gone a full week. He wanted to be sure she had his travel arrangements under control. Also, he needed to make the most of the time he had in the office next week. Scheduling had to be flawless. And he had to have everything that would need doing while he was in Australia effectively delegated.

Twice during that meeting, she caught him looking at her legs. This was not good—especially since she found she *liked* to have him looking at her legs.

Something definitely had to be done.

Saturday morning, she took action. She found a dingy little shop in a part of SA where she would never run into anyone she knew. The brawny, heavily tattooed guy behind the desk offered a nice range of cubic zirconia engagement and wedding rings. She chose a fat emerald-cut solitaire in a faux-platinum setting. It looked impressive—and real—on her finger, the price was right and the fake stone was really, really big and sparkly.

She took the ring home. Monday, before she went to the office, she slipped it onto her ring finger.

An hour and ten minutes later, when the elevator doors slid wide and Dax stepped off, the art assistant, two associate editors and Lin were gathered in an admiring circle around Zoe's desk.

Dax wore dark glasses. And even though Zoe couldn't see his eyes, he looked at least as tired and cranky as he had the Monday before. Had he been with Faye all weekend? If so, the woman must be insatiable. He looked drained of energy—and probably bodily fluids, as well.

"What's going on?" he groused. "Why aren't you people working? There's a planning meeting at ten in the conference room downstairs."

"Dax." Lin answered for all of them. "We know. We actually do get your memos. And after we get them, we read them."

He made a growly sort of sound low in his throat. "I'll expect at least five solid ideas from each of you. And Zoe, where's my coffee?"

Lin gave her a big smile. "Zoe, it's so beautiful. Seriously, I'm beyond happy for you." She winked so fast that only Zoe could have seen it and added archly, "On more than one level." She turned to go. The others dispersed with her.

Zoe grabbed the coffee she'd picked up on the way in and held it out to him. "Venti, bold and black. Good morning, Dax."

He took the coffee. "What's beautiful? Why is Lin happy for you?"

She held up her other hand and wiggled her fingers. The fake diamond glittered in a satisfyingly blinding fashion. "Johnny proposed," she announced on a happy sigh. "And I told him yes."

He took the lid off his coffee and stared down into it. Even though the sunglasses obscured his eyes, she assumed he was checking to make sure she hadn't slipped a little half and half in there or something. He sniffed at the contents and then demanded darkly, "Who's Johnny?"

She arranged her expression into a thoughtful frown. "Didn't I tell you about Johnny?"

"Not one word."

"Oh, I can't believe I never mentioned Johnny." She released another gusty sigh. "What can I say about Johnny?" She waved the hand with the ring on it. Flashes of refracted light bounced off the acoustical tile ceiling. "I met him at Stanford. Years ago. He's from a really old and important California family. He moved to San Antonio last fall. We've been dating—

both seriously and exclusively. Saturday, he asked me to be his wife."

Dax winced as he took off the sunglasses. "Well, give Johnny my congratulations. He's a fortunate man." He squinted at her. She couldn't tell if he was disappointed that they weren't ever having sex after all. Or if he just had a really bad hangover.

She beamed. "Yes, he's a lucky man. And I'm a happy, happy woman." She tried to look deeply in love as well as sexually sated.

His brow crinkled. "So does this mean you'll be giving me notice?"

She blinked. "Notice? Of course not. I intend to work for you for years and years."

He reminded her drily, "That is, if you pass your two-week review."

She brushed a curl of red hair back over her shoulder. "You know I will. Already, after one week, you can't function without me. And Johnny knows I love my new job. He would never ask me to quit."

"Johnny sounds like a real prize," he remarked with absolutely no inflection.

"Oh, he is, he is."

"In fact, he almost sounds too good to be true."

She didn't miss a beat. "He does, doesn't he? But he is very real. A man of flesh and blood, of—"

"Zoe?"

"Hmm?"

"Don't overplay it." He gave her one of those looks, both patient and all-knowing. Was he on to her little deception—already, when she'd barely begun it?

Surely not.

She smiled at him, a sweet smile. Angelic, even.

"All right, Dax. I'll do my best to keep my unbounded, ecstatic happiness to myself."

"Excellent. We need to prep for the meeting."

"The caterers from the bakery should be here by nine-thirty."

"Good. Give me ten minutes to pull myself together. We'll do a quick once-over of what has to be covered before we go down."

"I'm ready."

He shook his head. "Are you always so eager on a Monday morning?"

She beamed. "I'm young, I'm in love and I've got a great job."

"Ugh." He put his dark glasses back on. "That does it. I absolutely forbid you to smile again until at least 11 a.m."

"I live to serve." She mugged an exaggerated frown.

"There. That's more like it."

During the first three days of that week, Zoe made up a lot of stuff about Johnny—most of it on the spot when someone would ask her a question about him and she would have to produce an answer. Later, at home alone in the evening, she would open her "Johnny" file and add in whatever new information she'd fabricated about the new love of her life. It worked out well. She made up stuff and then she made sure she remembered what she'd said.

Johnny, as it turned out, was allergic to strawberries. His last name was Schofield—of the Mendocino Schofields. He traveled a lot, taking care of various "family interests." He loved long walks on the beach and quiet nights at home and he was an accomplished horseman.

He had moss-green eyes and dark gold hair that Zoe loved to run her fingers through. He was tender and loving, a good listener. He truly was the perfect man.

Well, except for the fact that he didn't exist.

Wednesday afternoon, as they were going over Dax's travel checklist for the last time, Zoe caught him yet again looking at her legs. She went right on with her rundown of his itinerary. There was no law that said he couldn't look.

She felt much more relaxed around him now. More confident in her ability to resist his considerable charm and powerful sex appeal. Johnny, as it turned out, had been just what she needed to help her keep her priorities in order.

Her big fake engagement diamond glittered at her, reminding her that she knew what she wanted and she would not be distracted from what mattered in her life. She smiled a soft, contented smile. She was keeping this job and she was going to be the best editorial assistant there was. Eventually, she might move on to become an editor in her own right.

Or, if Dax was willing to pay her enough to continue as his assistant, she would consider a new title of Executive Secretary to the Editor-in-Chief. And the fat paycheck that went with it.

She was going to go far at *Great Escapes*. But all in good time.

Thursday, with Dax on his way to Australia, she dug into the slush pile. She wanted to get caught up on the unagented submissions, get them logged and categorized by the time he returned.

She liked reading slush. She found she could pick

out the stories with potential. Those she flagged so Dax would be sure to give them a more careful look.

Reading slush also helped her to get ideas of her own. It inspired her to think in terms of what kinds of stories and features she might contribute to *Great Escapes*. It never hurt to plan ahead, to start preparing for the day when coming up with a story might become part of her job.

Sunday, the Fourth of July, she went out to the ranch again. She got there at eleven in the morning and stayed for the fireworks after dark. She had a great time, enjoyed the meal and the family conversation, and didn't once want to burst into tears because of some thoughtless remark her dad had made.

Monday at noon, she slipped off the fake diamond she'd put on that morning and met her sister Abilene for lunch at the Riverwalk. They split a turkey and mozzarella panini and Zoe talked about how much she loved her new job, while Abilene tried hard to stay upbeat.

Back in January, Abilene had won an important fellowship to co-design a children's center in collaboration with a certain world-famous architect. Now, months later, the project was on hold for some reason that was unclear to Abilene.

At least she'd managed to get some temporary work, thanks to Javier Cabrera. Javier owned Cabrera Construction and had been kind enough to take Abilene under his wing, hiring her to do some drafting for him and also to help him out at the construction sites of a couple of houses he was building.

Javier's relationship to the Bravo family was complicated, to say the least. But Abilene didn't seem to care about the family issues. She really liked Javier and appreciated that he'd put her on his payroll until the fellowship came through.

"If it ever does," Abilene said with a heavy sigh. "By now, I'm beginning to wonder. And I am beyond frustrated with the whole situation."

They agreed it was pretty ironic, actually. Always in the past, Abilene was the one who knew what she wanted from life and stayed happy and focused, working toward her goals. Now, Zoe was the one doing work that she loved. And Abilene was feeling powerless, trying to decide what she ought to do now: start looking for fulltime work. Or keep waiting in hopes that the fellowship would finally come through.

Dax returned Thursday morning. He called Zoe in first thing and they had a two-hour huddle, catching up, organizing priorities for the next couple of days.

When she stood to return to her desk, he said, "It's good to be back, Zoe. I missed you. Lulu doesn't read my mind anywhere near as well as you do."

It was a huge compliment. She clutched her laptop to her chest and tried not to look as dewy-eyed and thrilled as she felt. "Good. It was always my plan to become indispensable."

"And I'm beginning to believe your plan is working." They shared a long look—too long. He blinked first. "So, how's it going with Johnny?"

She almost asked, *Who?* But by some minor miracle, she caught herself in time. "He's…wonderful. In, uh, New York for a couple days. Left this morning, as a matter of fact. Some Wall Street deal, I think."

"Ah."

They looked at each other some more.

Get a grip, Zoe. Get it firm and get it now. "Well, okay, then. I'll just…go on back to my desk."

He nodded and reached for the phone. Twenty minutes later, he was on his way to a meeting. And another after that. The meetings went on until two.

At two-thirty, he went to work finishing the Spotlight on the Australian trip, locking himself in his office, only accepting calls if something absolutely couldn't wait. He stayed until after seven, and she stayed, too, just in case he might need anything while he pushed through to his deadline.

When he left, he asked her to look over what he'd written, just for grammar and punctuation. She said she would be happy to and tried not to let him see how ridiculously pleased and honored she felt.

She took the piece home with her and read it eagerly over take-out pot stickers and fried rice, red pencil within reach. It was really good. But then, his Spotlights always were. He had a master's in Journalism from Yale. More than that, though, he was a fine writer. He wrote with authority, but in an easy conversational style. He made you feel like you were there, with him, no matter how distant or exotic the locale.

In the morning, she emailed him back the manuscript. As she was leaving him after the usual huddle, she told him the Aussie holiday Spotlight was excellent.

He arched a brow. "No changes?"

She gave him a slow smile. They both knew the question was a test. He hadn't asked her to do an edit. "Three or four typos. I corrected them."

"Good. Thank you."

"Anytime."

"Do you realize that it's been over two weeks since you started and we've yet to get to that review?"

She shrugged. "It's been a busy time."

He agreed. "It's always busy around here."

She suggested, "Maybe…next week?"

"How about right now?"

Her stomach lurched, which was absurd. He was happy with her work. He'd made that abundantly clear. She had nothing to worry about.

"All right." She settled back down into the club chair. Her palms were actually sweating. She had to resist the need to rub them on her skirt. What was her problem? They both knew he was going to offer her a permanent job.

Didn't they?

He said, dark eyes knowing, "Zoe, are you nervous?"

She considered lying. She'd made up a fiancé, for heaven's sake. To lie about being anxious should be nothing next to that. But then, in the end, she told the truth. "Yeah." She let out a careful breath. "Whew. It's crazy, because I know I'm doing a terrific job for you. But I *am* nervous."

"Why?" He was looking at her so steadily. With real interest. Maybe more interest than he ought to have in his assistant—his *engaged* assistant. She wished he would *stop* looking at her that way.

But he didn't.

And perversely, she loved that he didn't.

Her nervousness turned to something else. Something a lot like excitement.

She told the truth again. "I love this job. I've finally found something that suits me. There's never a dull moment. I can handle this job, but it doesn't bore me.

There's always something new, something to challenge me. I wake up in the morning and I look forward to going to work. Until *Great Escapes,* I never felt that way about anything—at least not for more than ten minutes or so."

"You want to stay."

"Didn't I just say that?"

"You did. And I'm glad you did." He stared at her some more. Her cheeks felt warm. She had this…glowing sensation, kind of fizzy and happy and so very lovely. "Now is the time I should tell you where your work falls short."

She wanted to be the best, which meant she had to be open to criticism, to ways she could improve. "Yes. Good idea."

"Well, I'm sorry."

"Uh." Alarm jangled through her. What was he trying to say? "You are?"

"Because your work *doesn't* fall short."

Her alarm turned to satisfaction. Was she grinning like an idiot? Probably. But so what? She worked damned hard and it was good to hear how he appreciated that.

He said, "You're a self-starter, but you have no problem asking for help when you need it. You take criticism well, and you make use of it. So far, I only have to tell you once when I want you to change something you're doing."

The fizzy, bright feeling was back. And getting stronger. He kept on looking at her. Admiringly. Almost hopefully. She stared at his mouth and wondered what his lips would feel like touching hers. She thought about how she really would like, someday, to find out.

And then the phone rang.

* * *

Dax didn't answer it. In fact, he had the thoroughly unreasonable urge to pick the damn thing up, rip the cord free of the jack and throw it hard against the wall.

For a minute there, he'd almost thought Zoe was about to make a move on him. And being human and male, he'd wanted her to. A lot.

Which made him pretty damn stupid now, didn't it? If the phone hadn't rung, if she *had* made a move on him, he would very likely have taken her up on it.

And then, one way or another, he would have ended up losing the best assistant he'd ever had—even better than Lin.

The phone rang a second time. And a third.

When Zoe started to rise, he said low, "Don't. The front desk can take a message."

She sank back into the chair, a slightly stunned look on her face, those very kissable lips of hers parted, breathless. She knew exactly what had almost happened.

Did she regret that it hadn't? He couldn't help but hope so.

The phone jangled once more. And then it was quiet.

Neither of them said a word. He was aware that the tension between them was dissipating, that the dangerous moment had passed. They would not become lovers. And he would not have to try to find someone to replace her.

He wasn't sure whether he was relieved.

Or furious.

Zoe started to lick her lips, caught herself doing it and made herself stop. Her heart was suddenly going a hundred miles an hour, just galloping away in her chest, like wild mustangs on steroids.

That had been close.

Too close. Lucky for her, the phone had rung. If not, she might have...

She cut that thought dead.

No. She wouldn't have. She had her priorities in order. The job was what counted. Yes, she had a thing for the boss. A minor thing, a totally get-overable thing, just like every other woman on the planet.

She would get past it. Over time, the attraction would fade by itself. And when it did, she would still be working at *Great Escapes*.

Dax started discussing her salary.

She had the sense of having passed some important test, of having chosen the job she loved over the man *everybody* loved. She knew she had made the best choice.

And yet, she still couldn't completely deny a certain sadness, a touch of tender melancholy. She caught her left hand with her right and turned the big, fake diamond idly back and forth as she and Dax discussed his expectations of her—and hers, of the job.

She knew what she wanted and she had it in her grasp: her dream career. And it—this, now—was only the beginning. She was going to go far. She knew it. She was absolutely certain of it. She could go to Sunday dinner at Bravo Ridge for the rest of her life and not care what thoughtless remarks her dad might toss off at her. The free spirit of the family was all grown up now, taking on a professional woman's responsibilities and loving every minute of it.

Uh-uh. She was not sad. Not sad in the least. She

would never know what it would feel like to kiss Dax Girard. And that was fine. It was right.

She had made her choice and she was at peace with it.

Chapter Three

The next week, on Thursday, Faye showed up again.

That time, Zoe acted fast. She jumped up and blocked the way to Dax's door. "Let me just check."

A slow sigh and then the sexy, husky voice. "If you insist."

"Have a seat. This won't take a minute."

Faye made an impatient sound low in her throat, but then she did go over and drop into one of the chairs by the enormous potted snake plant in the corner. Zoe turned and tapped on Dax's shut door.

"What?"

She opened it and stuck her head through. "Faye is here."

"Faye," he repeated blankly. Then he blinked. "Oh. Where?"

Zoe tipped her head toward the chair by the snake plant. "I'll show her in."

"No." He rose and came around the desk. "I'll come out there." Zoe moved aside and he emerged from his office. He aimed a practiced smile at the brunette. "Faye, I wasn't expecting you."

Faye stood up. "You ought to check your voice mail now and then."

He went to her. She reached to embrace him. He smoothly slid from her grasp, simultaneously taking one of her hands and tucking it around his forearm. "Let's go somewhere we can talk."

The Bambi eyes shone with tears. "Oh, Dax..."

He led her to the elevator. They got in and the doors slid shut. Zoe heard the faint whoosh and lurch as the car started down.

Was he dumping Faye? It sure looked like it.

Zoe didn't know what she felt about that. A little sorry for Faye, maybe, which surprised her. A little annoyed with Dax.

How old was he anyway, thirty-five or thirty-six? Old enough to stop jumping from one woman's bed to the next. If he didn't watch it, he'd end up ancient and wrinkled, wearing a satin bathrobe, with a blonde young enough to be his granddaughter on his arm.

That image made her wince. And then she couldn't help but laugh. Dax was Dax. A woman was only begging for trouble if she started expecting him to change his ways.

Dax really hated it when a woman cried.

When a woman cried, it made him feel crappy and powerless. Tears were the one thing a man had no idea how to fight. You couldn't win an argument with tears. You couldn't punch a tear's lights out.

You just had to sit there and try to think of the right

thing to say, try *not* to make promises you had no intention of keeping.

He took Faye to a bar not far from the office. A nice, dark, quiet place where few of his associates ever went. He guided her toward a booth in the back.

Business was pretty slow. The bartender came over and took their drink order. Faye wanted a Cosmopolitan; Dax just had club soda. He had work to do back at the office and he couldn't afford to be fuzzy-headed when he returned.

The drinks arrived. The bartender went off to mind his own business.

Faye sipped her pretty pink drink and sobbed. She told him she loved him.

He felt like a jerk.

He probably was a jerk, but that wasn't the issue right now. The issue was Faye and how it was over with her and how he had to get her to see that, to look on the bright side, to remember what a good time they'd had and realize she was ready to move on.

Faye kept on sobbing. He didn't have any tissues handy, so he passed her a cocktail napkin.

She delicately dabbed her wet eyes with it. "You're such a jerk."

He wasn't offended. It was only what he'd just been thinking himself. He spoke gently, "Come on, Faye. Don't. It's going to be all right."

She sniffled and delicately dabbed at her eyes some more, trying to mop up the tears without smearing her makeup. "I knew. From the beginning. It's not as if I wasn't warned. Love never lasts with you."

Love. He hadn't mentioned love. Not once. He kept love strictly out of his vocabulary when he dated a woman. It was ingrained in him, a nonnegotiable rule. And he never broke a nonnegotiable rule.

He said, "I've enjoyed the time we've spent together."

She sniffed, sobbed, swallowed. "Enjoyed. Past tense. Oh, Dax…"

"You're young and so beautiful…"

"Is that supposed to make everything all right? Well, it doesn't, okay? It just doesn't."

He tried to think of the next thing to say. He was usually reasonably glib when it got to this point. But he didn't feel glib today. He only felt…sorry. Really, really sorry. "I'm sorry, Faye. Truly."

She dabbed at her mascara some more. "Sorry doesn't do me any good."

"I know."

"They say that you end up friends with most of your ex-girlfriends."

"I like to think that's true."

"Well, I don't want to be friends, Dax. I really don't." She picked up her Cosmo and downed it in one long swallow. Then she set the stemmed glass down hard. "I guess that's it. Goodbye, Dax." She slid out of the booth and headed for the door.

After Faye was gone, Dax stayed in the booth alone for a while, sipping his club soda, thinking about how he hated ending it with a woman. Endings were depressing. He liked beginnings a lot better.

Too bad beginnings never lasted. Too bad the nature of a beginning was to move along toward another ending. And the only way to stop the endings was to stop enjoying the beginnings.

Unless a man decided to settle down, to find someone he could share a lifetime of middles with, so their story had no end. But a lifetime of middles wasn't on his horizon. He was never getting married again.

For no particular reason, he thought of Zoe. Of her too-good-to-be-true fiancé who had yet to show his face around the office. Of what a great assistant she was. Of how he would never have to end it with her—well, except when she moved up the next rung of the editorial ladder, which was bound to happen, and probably sooner than later.

That would be a pain in the ass, trying to find another assistant.

But he would manage it somehow. There was going to be no holding Zoe back, he knew that.

At least when he lost her there wouldn't be any crying, no groping for the right words and coming up with only hollow clichés. She would be happy when he lost her. He would be resigned, would do his best to keep her at the magazine. If he couldn't have her guarding his office door forever, at least *Great Escapes* could get the benefit of her talent and drive.

And that was as good as it got.

In the end, a guy had to be grateful for small favors.

"So I have this idea..." Zoe said the following Tuesday, as they were winding down the morning huddle.

He'd been expecting this. Of course, she had an idea. She'd been working for him for just four weeks and already organized his slush pile. She knew the plan for the next seven issues backward and forward, had a great instinct for what would work for the magazine and what wouldn't. When she flagged a piece for him, he knew it was something he had to make time to take a look at.

She was on her feet by then, clutching her laptop, the absurdly large diamond on her engagement ring twinkling at him. "It's…for a Spotlight." She actually sounded hesitant, which rather charmed him. Zoe rarely sounded nervous about anything. Even when she wasn't sure what she was doing, she took care to project confidence. "I was thinking we could discuss it—I mean, when you've got a spare moment or two."

"I'm listening. Tell me about it now."

"Well, all right." She dropped back into her chair again, set the laptop on her knees. "I'm thinking 'Spotlight on a Shoestring'—because of the economy, you know? That people are looking for value in everything they do, including when they travel. I'm thinking Mexico—and no, do not give me that look. Not Cancún or Puerto Vallarta. I'm thinking of something a little more out of the way."

"Like?"

"Southern Mexico, the state of Chiapas near the Guatemalan border. San Cristóbal de las Casas, to be specific."

"You're kidding."

She sat straighter and got that pugnacious look. He really liked that look. "I am one-hundred-percent serious. It's a great value. Four-star hotels at a hundred bucks a night. Wonderful food at really low prices and a fabulous central market where you can get amazing deals on local arts and crafts. Biking, birdwatching. Rainforest all around, filled with thousands of exotic plants and animals. Spectacular Mayan ruins…"

He put up a finger. "Two words."

"What?"

"Armed insurgents."

She wrinkled her adorable nose at him. "I had a feeling you would say that."

He knew a lot about Mexico. But then, he knew a lot about many places. "They're called the Zapatistas, Zoe. And they're nothing to fool with."

"Most of the trouble was back in the nineties. Things are better now."

"But is better good enough?"

"It is, yes. I'm sure it's safe. Yes, the Zapatistas are in a war against the Mexican state, against globalization. But it's mostly a nonviolent conflict. My research tells me that travelers are safer in and around San Cristóbal than in just about any major American city. As long as they behave respectfully and don't take pictures without asking first." She produced a memory stick. "Here's what I have. I've tried to cover everything—what to pack, what to see, where to stay, how to get there."

"A spreadsheet for projected costs?"

"That, too."

He held out his hand. "I'll give it a look."

Her sleek brows drew together. He knew she was considering working on him a little more before she turned him loose with what she'd worked up. But apparently she decided against that, decided to let the work she'd done speak for itself. He very much approved of that.

She rose and passed him the stick. "Can't ask for more."

That evening, he read her proposal. And the next morning, when they went over his calendar, he told her what he thought.

"I like it. We're going to do it."

She gasped and those blue eyes lit up, bright as stars. "You mean it?"

He nodded.

"Yes!" In her excitement, she almost dropped her laptop. It slid off her knees. She lurched to rescue it and whacked her hand hard against the side of his desk. The enormous diamond made a loud cracking sound. Something plopped to the floor.

They stared at each other.

She let out a wild little laugh. "Oops." She had her laptop stabilized on her knees and she was clutching her left hand with her right. She pressed her lips together as a scarlet flush rushed up her creamy cheeks. "Uh, sorry."

Was she hurt? "Are you okay?"

"Uh, yeah. Fine. Perfect." She pulled the ring off her finger—but carefully, keeping it out of his sight. "I think I, um, bent the setting on my ring a little."

"Sounded to me like you broke the damn thing."

The flush on her pretty face intensified. Her cheeks were now cherry-red. "No, no. Of course not." Trying not to be obvious about it, she scanned the floor around her chair.

He pushed back his own chair and looked under his desk.

Near his left shoe, half of her engagement diamond sparkled at him. He bent and picked it up.

When he straightened, she was staring at him. The look on her face was absolutely priceless. He leaned across the desk and held the broken stone out to her.

She took it from him. "Uh, thanks."

"It appears that Johnny will be buying you another ring. Tell him not to be such a cheap bastard this time."

She looked as if she wished she could sink right through the floor. But Zoe was not one to be cowed by a little thing like abject humiliation. She pulled herself together and jumped to Johnny's defense. "I'll have you know that Johnny is not cheap—and this…" She looked down at the two halves of her supposed engagement diamond. "It's nothing."

He arched a brow but kept his mouth shut. He was thoroughly enjoying himself. Hadn't had this much fun in a very long time.

She backpedaled madly, that quick brain of hers firing on all cylinders. "A…duplicate, a fake. I had it made."

"Made?"

"Yes. Made—you know, because I was nervous. Muggings are…simply rampant these days."

Simply rampant, huh? "No kidding?"

She fisted the broken ring in her palm and sat up straighter, flicking a thick swatch of that gorgeous red hair back over her shoulder. "Yes, well. Ahem…where were we?"

He debated whether to torture her some more or move on. In the end, he took pity on her. "The San Cristóbal Spotlight."

She swallowed, nodded, eager to talk more about her proposal—and to put the embarrassing incident with the ring behind her. "I'm so pleased, Dax. I can't tell you how much this means."

"I've been thinking about what month we should use it." With relish, he delivered the bombshell. "I'm thinking January."

Her mouth dropped open again. He really did enjoy catching her off-guard. "B-but January is already locked in."

Yes, it was. Spotlights, along with the rest of the

magazine, were planned and scheduled nine months to a year in advance.

"I run this magazine. And if I say we go to Chiapas and not Greece for January, then that's where we go."

"But you're leaving for Greece in a week and a half. I have the travel arrangements all set up."

"Then you will change them. A little spontaneity is good now and then."

"But…what if I can't get that fabulous hotel?"

"You'll find another fabulous hotel. I have faith in your ingenuity and resourcefulness." He sat back in his chair and waited for her to confess what was really bothering her.

"But I…" She had her free hand folded over the one with the broken ring in it and both of them resting on her shut laptop. She stared down—at her hands, at the laptop? He couldn't tell which. Her slim shoulders were slumped. She almost might have been praying.

"Zoe." He spoke softly. "You what?"

The red head lifted, the shoulders went back and the blue eyes gleamed. "I was hoping, well, that it would be a little later. At least not for a few months. Not until, um, after the rainy season ends."

"I don't see a little rain as that much of a problem."

"Daily, Dax. It comes down in buckets."

"I know my weather patterns. It rains hard, but mostly just in the afternoon."

So much for the rainy season. She let that go and cast about for another excuse to postpone the trip. "But I, well, if you could only wait until I've been working for you longer, until…" Words deserted her.

He didn't let her off the hook. "What? Tell me."

"Oh, please." Her heated gaze accused him. "You know. I *know* you know."

"You still have to say it. That's how it works. You have to speak up and say what you want. Come on. Look at it this way, if you don't get what you ask for, at least you'll know you put yourself out there, that you did everything you could to make it happen."

She sat up even straighter. "Fine. All right. I want you to wait to do the Spotlight on San Cristóbal until you're ready to take me along as your assistant, instead of one of the associates. That's what I want, okay? I want to go."

He rested his elbows on the chair arms and steepled his fingers. Yeah, he was playing this, stringing it along to enjoy her honest excitement, her clear desire to be directly involved in the feature she had just proposed. Most of the time, she was careful around him, she guarded that light in her eyes from him. She tried to keep things all business.

And he respected that, he really did. Still, it was gratifying for him, to listen to her speak with heat, with passion. To see her eagerness, her enthusiasm, her willingness to push for what she wanted, to try to get him to give her a chance, to let her take the next step.

She glared at him. "Just tell me. Just give me an answer. Will you wait for a few months to do *my* Spotlight?"

"No."

Her sweet, soft mouth trembled as she pressed her lips together to keep herself from calling him a thoroughly inappropriate name. He liked that about her, too. She had passion, but she also kept herself in hand. She took care not to step over the line.

"Well." A slow, deep breath. A toss of that flame-colored hair. "Fine, then. You were right, I needed to ask. At least I'll never kick myself because I didn't even try."

"I don't think you'll kick yourself at all."

She blinked. And then she gasped. She got what he was hinting at. "You're serious?"

"Yes. It's early, I know. But you learn fast. I think you're ready. You'll get to prove yourself."

"I'm going with you?" Breathless, heartbreakingly hopeful.

"Yes, Zoe. I'm doing your Chiapas trip instead of the one to Mykonos. I'm leaving Monday, August second. And you are going with me."

Chapter Four

"Have you made the reservations for Mexico yet?" Dax asked the next morning as he stepped out of the elevator.

Of course she had. She'd worked late the day before, getting everything set up. She handed him his coffee. "Yes. Mexicana Airlines. One stopover in Mexico City and then on to the international airport at Tuxtla Gutiérrez, the capital city of the state of Chiapas. We can get a taxi from there to…" She let the words trail off as she saw that he was shaking his head. "Is there a problem?"

He took the lid off his coffee, sniffed it the way he always did and then enjoyed a careful sip. "Cancel the flight."

She blinked. "Excuse me?"

"How are you in small planes?"

"With enough Dramamine, anything is possible, but—"

"Good. I'm going to fly us."

Not in her plan. Not in the least. "Dax…"

"Don't argue. Just do it."

"If I could only make one little point…"

"You're boring me, Zoe."

"Too bad. I intend to make my point and my point is that readers like to know how you got there—on a commercial flight, just the way that they will. Especially since this is supposed to be a budget destination."

His smile was annoyingly smug. "Now you know more than I do about what readers want in a Spotlight?"

"I didn't say that."

"But you sure as hell are thinking it. Cancel the reservation. We're going to have some fun."

The way he said that kind of scared her. "I, um, didn't know you were a pilot."

He gave her a look of endless patience. "I may be in magazine publishing now, but I spent years adventuring in the wilds, from Borneo to the South Pole."

As if she didn't know that. "Yes, but—"

"I've been flying small planes since I was too young to drive a car. Cancel the flights."

She ground her teeth together and reminded herself that he was the boss, that she was very grateful to him for giving her this chance when she'd been his assistant for only a month. "Yes, Dax. All right."

"I love it when you're obsequious. It happens so seldom. And guess what?"

"I have no idea."

"I've already found our photographer." He paused, sipped more coffee.

"I'm listening." No, she had no illusions it was going to be her.

And it wasn't. "I called Ramón Esquevar. He'll be in Guatemala next week and he's promised to meet us in San Cristóbal."

Okay, she was totally impressed. She sighed. She couldn't help it. Esquevar was world-class. His photographs appeared in *Time* and *National Geographic*. She'd always hoped someday she might meet him. Now she would get to watch him work.

Dax was grinning at her. "You're speechless."

She let her smile bloom wide. "Esquevar. I can hardly believe it. That's fabulous."

"We got lucky. The timing just happened to be right for him." He spotted her ring finger, where a ring that looked exactly like the one she had broken the day before glittered, big and bright. "That was fast."

She kept on smiling. Let him think what he wanted. She'd gone back to the same shop last night, got there just before it closed. The tattooed shopkeeper had dug up another ring for her—even given her a discount after she gave him a hard time for selling shoddy goods.

Dax sipped his coffee and watched her for a minute, no doubt waiting for her to confess that there was no Johnny and there never had been.

She did no such thing. The deception might be a little frayed around the edges. But it still did the job, still made it clear to Dax—to *both* of them—that she was off-limits to him as a potential bed partner.

Finally, he growled at her, "What are you grinning about? Why aren't you working?" and turned and disappeared into his office.

The rest of that week and the one that followed were hectic. There were a thousand and one things to do before they could be ready to go. And the time line to get everything in order was scarily short. Preparations for the Spotlight trips usually took months of careful planning. But not this time. Dax had decided they were changing everything up. And Dax, after all, was the boss.

Over a stolen hour for lunch the Friday before they left, Lin said it was his nature. "Things go too smoothly for too long, he can't stand it. He needs challenge, a little crisis theater, some spice in his life."

Zoe sipped her iced tea. "You know he's flying us?"

"Why not? He owns three or four planes. Might as well use one of them."

"A small plane, he said. A single-engine plane. Ugh."

"Look on the bright side. Commercial flights are a zoo these days, planes breaking down, the nightmare of security checkpoints. With an airline, you could land in Mexico City and never leave."

"We have to stop just over the border at Nuevo Laredo anyway, and deal with customs. The checklist of papers we have to carry and file is endless. We even had to get third-party liability insurance from a Mexican company."

Lin waved a hand. "Travel's a pain, it's true."

"That's not what I'm talking about. I love to travel, under any circumstances. I love luxury destinations. And I don't mind roughing it."

"But you hate small planes, is that it?"

"No, I can take a small plane. I get a little motion sickness, but I have the pills to handle that."

Lin shrugged. "Then what is it? Is Johnny upset that you'll be gone for a week?"

"No. Of course not. Johnny…supports me. Completely."

"Then what is the problem?"

Zoe thought about Dax. His honed razor of a mind, his hot body. His gorgeous bedroom eyes that could look so low-lidded and sensual, but somehow always saw way too much. She loved her job. She would not lose it. And she had this feeling lately that Dax had set out to purposely tempt her.

Just the two of them, in a small plane. It seemed… dangerous—though, really, how could it be? He would be flying the damn thing. No way would he have a chance to try convincing her of the benefits of joining the mile-high club.

And even if he did break his own rule and make a pass, well, he wasn't going to get anywhere with her. She had her priorities in order. Ending up in bed with Dax was at the very top of her list—her *never-to-do* list.

"Zoe. Yoo-hoo. You're zoning out on me here…."

Zoe blinked away her worries and pasted on a bright smile. "Sorry. You're right. The small plane thing is fine. It's perfect. The whole trip is perfect. I don't know why I'm complaining. I'm going to meet Ramón Esquevar. It's my first Spotlight, one I came up with myself, and I'm thrilled to be going. There is no problem. No problem at all."

They were in the air at eight in the morning on Monday, the second of August. The four-seater Cessna 400 Corvalis TT—for Twin Turbocharged—was top-of-the-line among single-engine aircraft, Dax explained. Zoe thought it was rather like sitting in a big, comfortable luxury sedan—a sedan that sailed the clear blue sky and had an instrument panel instead of a dashboard.

There was plenty of room in back for the clothing and equipment they would need, and then some. Zoe had taken her Dramamine and was feeling pleasant and relaxed as she looked down on the San Antonio sprawl below them. She watched as it faded away behind them.

"This baby has a cruising speed of two-hundred thirty-five knots," Dax told her with the pride men always seem to have in their big, expensive toys. "We'll be in Nuevo Laredo in no time."

And they were. They checked in with customs and were cleared for takeoff again an hour later. Because the Cessna 400 had a ginormous gas tank, they could now go all the way to their destination airport at Tuxtla Gutiérrez. That would take another five or six hours.

"I can't wait," Zoe said drily. But she would have to. She'd been careful not to go overboard on the morning coffee and to visit the ladies room at Nuevo Laredo. But even with that, she had a feeling she was going to be very grateful to touch down and race for the nearest *el baño*.

For a while, Zoe watched the land flow away from them below and snapped a few random pictures of the starkly beautiful desert rock formations with her lightweight Nikon D90, which she considered the best possible all-around camera there was.

Yes, she had more expensive cameras. She had a nice trust fund and could afford to indulge herself. But for most situations, the D90 and a couple of good lenses were all she ever needed.

Dax seemed happy as a kid in a big candy store. He extolled yet more of the virtues of the Cessna 400.

"Safety is a top priority with Cessna. Every exterior surface—fuselage and wings *and* the flight controls—is embedded with lightning mesh. You never have to worry about a lightning strike. Also, they install static wicks on the back edge of the wings and elevator, which means static buildup is discharged safely without affecting function or disrupting other electrical systems."

"That really puts my mind at rest," she told him drily.

"I knew it would. I love to fly. My uncle Devon, the family ne'er-do-well, taught me. He had a ranch near Amarillo."

"Being a rancher makes a guy a ne'er-do-well?"

"To my father, it did. He and my uncle were the last of the Girard line. My father expected my uncle Devon to do what all Girards have done. Because a Girard comes from money—and is fully expected to do his part making more money. My uncle refused to follow the plan."

She knew that *Great Escapes* was not a huge moneymaker. "So you're kind of like your uncle, huh?"

The dig didn't even faze him. "Yeah, guess I am. But I do understand money and I know whom to hire to make me more of it, so I can afford to indulge myself in my passion for travel and in my magazine."

"And in your airplanes and expensive cars and designer motorcycles."

"Yes, exactly. And still my fortune just keeps on growing."

"Not that you're bragging about that or anything."

He slanted her a glance. "You really should be more impressed with me, you know."

"Sorry, I'll work on that."

"And where was I?"

"Your ne'er-do-well rancher uncle who taught you to fly."

"That's it. Now and then, I got to go visit Uncle Devon. He started teaching me to fly when I was eight."

She rested her camera in her lap. "Eight, yikes! That shouldn't be legal."

"But it is. You can start to learn at any age. You just have to be tall enough to reach the controls."

"But you grew up on the East Coast, right?"

"We had homes all over the world. But we lived in an apartment on Park Avenue. And we had a house upstate—not that we ever visited there after my mother died. The house had been hers. My dad couldn't bear to part with it, but he couldn't stand to be there either. He never admitted it, but I knew it brought back too many memories of her."

"You have brothers and sisters?"

He shook his head. "I was an only child."

It seemed strange, thinking of Dax as a child—with a mom and a dad and a ne'er-do-well uncle. She chuckled. "You know, Dax, I can't picture you with a mom—or a dad, for that matter. Then again, everybody has one of each, right?"

He shrugged. "I hardly remember my mom. I was five when she died."

She thought of her own mom, of Aleta's innate goodness, her fierce love for each and every one of her nine children. "How sad for you," she told him softly.

He sent her another glance and a faint smile in response, then turned his gaze back to the wide sky ahead.

The weather was perfect. Zoe put her camera away and settled back in the comfy leather seat. Through the windscreen, the sky was endless, not a cloud in sight, a gorgeous expanse of baby blue. The steady drone of the engine lulled her and the Dramamine made her sleepy. She let her eyes drift shut.

For a long time, she drifted, dreaming in snatches, coming slightly awake to the smooth, steady drone of the Cessna's engine, to awareness that she was on her way to the jungles of Mexico with her hot-guy boss, Dax Girard, that she was going to meet Ramón Esquevar, taste some of the best coffee in the world, visit the ancient Mayan villages of San Juan Chamula and Zinacantán. She would tell herself she really ought to wake up, act like a decent assistant, make a little conversation, at least.

But Dax didn't seem to mind if she slept. He flew the plane and left her alone and she felt so peaceful. Inevitably, after a few moments of wakefulness, she would fade back into her own pleasant oblivion again.

What woke her, finally, was the turbulence. All of a sudden, they were dipping and dropping, literally lurching through the sky.

Her eyes popped open as a volley of hail beat at the windscreen.

It was dark. When had that happened?

She glanced over at Dax. "Is it nighttime?"

He shook his head. "Just a squall. But a wild one. I've been trying to get above it, but it's not working. And we seem to be in a dead space. I'm getting no response on the radio. Check your restraint. In a minute, I'm going to see if I can get below this."

Check your restraint? She was not reassured. Still, she tugged on the belt to make sure it was fastened securely.

More hail pelted the plane and the wind screamed

like the end of the world. They kept rising and drop-ping—hard—as if they'd actually hit some physical object, though she knew they hadn't, that it was only the racing wind currents.

They would bottom out, the small plane shaking as if grabbed and pummeled by the hand of an angry god. And then they would rise again, only to fall once more.

Rain came—buckets of it. Beyond the cabin, she saw nothing but darkness and horizontal walls of water coming at them, racing by. The wind wailed and they lurched and bounced. The restraint held her in the seat, but in back, she could hear the strapped-in equip-ment. Even tied down with a cargo net, it was banging around, hitting the fuselage, battering the backs of the rear seats.

And the stomach-churning drops continued. The plane bounced like a ball, a toy tossed between the cruel hands of a madman.

Still, she refused to believe that they wouldn't get through this. She was twenty-five years old. She had a wonderful family, a father who drove her nuts but who she knew adored her. A mother who had never wavered in her devotion, her loving support.

She'd finally found work she could do for years and only get better at it, never get bored. She didn't have to be the slacker of the family anymore. Her whole life lay ahead of her, beckoning. It was all coming together, and it was going to be so good.

Surely, it couldn't be snatched away now.

Dax kept trying to raise a response on the radio. Nothing. He spoke to her once. "Next time, I swear, we'll fly commercial."

He mouthed their coordinates into the unresponsive radio and yet again gave the distress signal.

The plane started down. At the last second, she saw that he had found a bare space in the wall of black and green below them. A very small clearing in the dense, never-ending forest—surely, that tiny cleared space was much too small for a landing.

She said what she was thinking, "Oh, God, Dax. Too small, too small."

He didn't answer. He was kind of busy. They hurtled toward the minuscule clearing as the wind and the rain tried to rip them apart.

Her last thought before they reached the ground was, *I guess I won't be meeting Ramón Esquevar, after all.*

With a teeth-cracking bounce, they hit the ground. Dax couldn't keep the nose up. The propeller dug into the soggy, black earth. It dug and held, the engine screaming. Huge clods of dirt were flying everywhere.

And the plane was spinning, spinning, the jungle that rimmed the clearing whizzing by in a circle, so fast she thought she might throw up. She heard cracking, shattering sounds. Something hit the back of her seat hard enough to force all the breath from her lungs. And then something bopped her on the back of the head.

She cried out. And then she sighed.

As blackness rolled over her, she knew it was the end.

Chapter Five

"Zoe? Zoe, wake up." A hand slapped her cheek lightly. A delicate sting.

And her head hurt like crazy. She groaned, reached back, felt wetness. She opened her eyes, brought her hand in front of her face. Blood, but not much. She reached back a second time, probed the injury carefully. Already a goose egg was rising.

Goose eggs were good, she'd read somewhere, hadn't she? If the swelling was on the outside, you were less likely to end up with a subdural hematoma, which could be bad. Very, very bad.

"Zoe?"

She blinked. Dax was craning toward her from the other seat. He'd taken off his headphones and his chest was bare. He held his shirt to his forehead, on the left side. The shirt was soaked through with blood.

"Thank God," he said. "Zoe."

"We're not dead." Shè spoke in awe. It was a miracle. Impossible. And yet, somehow, true.

Dax retreated to his seat, tipped his head back and shut his eyes. He still held the bloody shirt to his head. Really, he didn't look so good. She realized he needed help. And she was just sitting there...

Blinking away the last of her dizziness, she went for the latch on her seat restraint. For a moment, she thought it was jammed, that somehow, in the landing, which had turned out to be something of a crash, it had been broken and stuck shut.

Panic tried to rise. She bit the inside of her cheek, focused on the sharp little pain, and worked at the latch some more.

A second later, it popped open.

She was out of the seat and ripping off her white shirt without even stopping to think about it. She wadded the cotton fabric into a ball and crouched over his seat. "Dax." She caught his chin with one hand. "Let me see..."

He lowered his hand and she saw the deep gash at his temple—the *really* deep gash. Beneath all that blood, she could see the ivory luster of bone.

And the blood? It was still flowing, lots of it, pulsing from the wound in great gouts. It ran down the side of his face, into his eyes.

"Here. Use this." She gave him her own shirt.

He dropped the blood-soaked one and put hers over the wound. Through the blood in his eyes, he looked at her in her bra and shorts. A corner of his mouth twitched in the faint hope of a smile. "I've got you with your shirt off, and I'm bleeding too hard to do a damn thing about it."

"I need a first aid kit."

"In the floor compartment behind your seat." He held her shirt to his head, but it was already soaking through, turning a bold, bright crimson.

"Keep the pressure on that. Good and firm."

"Right." He did as she instructed without a word of complaint, without giving her any argument. It was so unlike him to be docile. And that terrified her, brought the reality of their situation too sharply home.

The fuselage, amazingly, remained intact. They were reasonably safe inside. But outside the battered plane, the rain kept on coming, in buckets. Lightning flashed and thunder rumbled. The windscreen was a thick, pearly spiderweb of cracks, obscuring the world beyond. And the window in Dax's door was the same, but with a small jagged hole punched clean through it— just possibly caused by whatever had sliced his forehead open.

However, she could see well enough out the window in her door. Too bad visibility past the window was poor. Nothing but sheets of rain and, indistinctly, a wall of green where the jungle started.

Not now. Don't think about what's out there now....

She squeezed between the seats and had to spend several precious seconds tossing supplies, suitcases and equipment back toward the baggage area. Water bottles were scattered everywhere, broken loose from the case of them they'd brought along, rolling around on the floor. But finally, she got the area cleared. She was able to get the compartment open and take out a large, black canvas-covered bag with a white cross printed on the front.

"How you doing back there?" Dax asked. "Need help?"

"I'm on it. Just stay in your seat and keep the pressure on that wound." She cleared a space on one of the backseats and zipped the bag open. It was a really good kit—way beyond the basics. More like something a paramedic might carry. It even contained the necessary tools for sewing up a man's head.

I can do this. I took first aid. And then there was that survivalist training weekend she'd gone on once in her ongoing effort to prove to her dad that she was as good as any of the boys. They'd taught her how to stitch up a wound over that weekend. She remembered thinking at the time that she would never need to use that particular skill...

She sucked in a breath—and shook her head, hard. No. No negative thoughts could be allowed to creep in. She knew what she needed to do. And she knew how to do it.

Grabbing the kit, she scrambled between the front seats again. When she got up there, she set the kit, open, on the passenger side.

"Zoe?" He sounded worried.

"I'm right here. Keep the pressure against the wound. I know what I'm doing."

He made a low sound. A chuckle—or a groan? "Of course you do."

She smiled at that. Even now, with a gash the size of Texas on his forehead, he could manage to both tease and reassure her at the same time. She found the butterfly bandages and gazed at them longingly. If only they would do the trick.

But the wound was too deep. Maybe they could help to hold the edges together while she stitched him up.

She still wore her fake engagement ring. During the crash, the stone had scratched up the fingers to either side of it. She was clearly the lucky one. A few bruises, some scratches. A goose egg on the back of her head. No gash so deep the bone showed—and really, they were *both* lucky.

Lucky simply to be alive and in one piece. She had to remember that.

She yanked off the silly ring and shoved it into a pocket of her shorts. Then she rubbed disinfectant on her hands and laid out what she was going to need: the butterfly strips, tweezers, more disinfectant, sterile gloves, absorbable thread, scissors, the creepy little curved needle, the dressing she would use after, along with a tube of antibiotic ointment—and extra gauze. There was nothing to dull the pain of what she was about to do to him. Nothing stronger than acetaminophen—wait.

There was codeine. She almost kissed the little bottle of pills before she screwed off the cap.

"Dax, did you get knocked out, even for a few seconds during the crash?"

"Huh?"

"I'm afraid to give you a serious pain killer if you've been unconscious."

"No," he said. "Something sharp flew by and sliced my head open, that's all."

"Excellent." She took his free hand, dropped two of the pills into his palm, and closed his lean fingers around them. "Here."

"What are they?"

"Codeine."

"I don't think so. It doesn't hurt that much. Head wounds usually don't."

If it didn't hurt now, it would when she went to work on it. "Dax. Take the pills."

He blew out a breath, opened his mouth and tossed them in.

"Perfect. Thank you." She grabbed for one of the water bottles that had escaped the baggage area, and gave him a sip.

"More," he said low. She let him have the bottle. He drank half of it, then handed it back. He was eyeing the other seat: the scissors, the needle, the pile of white gauze, all so carefully laid out. "You're actually going to try and sew me up, huh?"

"That is the plan—and I'm going to do much more than try." She cleaned her hands again, then put on the gloves. "Okay, let's take another look…"

The console between the seats was in her way, but she lifted one knee and braced it on his seat to get in close. He tried to scoot over a little, to give her room to work—and gasped.

She frowned. "What? Your leg, too?"

"My ankle…" He hissed through his teeth, panting, getting through the pain. He reached toward it but got nowhere, with her practically on top of him. "I think it's just a sprain." He let his head drop to the seat rest again and swore low. "What a screwup. Bleeding all over the place—and I don't think I can walk."

"It's okay," she told him, not because it was true, but because there was nothing else to say. "The codeine will help with the pain and we'll deal with the ankle once we take care of your head."

He grunted, tried a grin but didn't quite make it. "Nurse Bravo, I'm at your mercy."

"Hmm. Could this be the right moment to hit you up for a raise?"

"Always working the angles."

"A girl's gotta do what a girl's gotta do. Now, let me see what I'm dealing with here...."

He lowered the bloody shirt from his forehead.

The blood flow had slowed, which was good. But then she had to clean and disinfect the injury thoroughly and that got the bleeding going again. She dabbed and poked and pressed at the gash and the surrounding tissue until she had it clear enough to work on.

The sewing-up took way too long. Each stitch had to be separate, so the whole thing wouldn't come apart if one happened to break. At least she found she did know what she was doing. During that delightful survivalist weekend, they'd made her practice doing stitches on a round steak, which she'd found thoroughly gross at the time. Who knew that someday she would be grateful for the experience?

Dax sat still beneath her hands. She knew it had to hurt, but he didn't make a sound.

She was sweating bullets by the end of it—from the stress, from the concentration, from the increasing sticky heat in the cabin. It was a great moment, when she finally set the scissors and needle aside. The dressing came next and that took no time at all.

"There," she said, snapping off the disposable gloves. "Done at last."

He tried to smile. "How do I look?"

"Rakish. All the girls will be after you. The scar is going to really wow them."

He grunted. He was probably thinking that he didn't need any more girls after him. But he didn't say it. He only whispered, "Thank you, Zoe."

She handed him the water bottle. "Drink." She grabbed one for herself, too, and took a big gulp.

He screwed the lid back on his slowly. "Don't know why I'm so exhausted."

She was repacking the first aid kit by then. "Maybe the crash landing. Maybe the loss of blood. Maybe the twelve stitches in your forehead."

"Maybe the codeine."

"Hmm. Could be that, too—I need to look at your ankle now."

His lower lip had a mutinous curl. "It's okay for now. I think the codeine is kicking in. I can hardly feel anything."

"Still, we can wrap it, for support, and you should get it elevated. Too bad we don't have any ice…"

"You're a pain in the ass, Zoe, you know that?"

"Flattering me will get you nowhere."

He grunted. "There should be a six-pack of instant ice pouches in the first aid kit—good for a whole twenty minutes each."

"Twenty minutes is better than nothing—and times six, that's a couple of hours. Every little bit helps." She dug out the box of cold packs, put the unzipped first aid kit on the cabin floor at her feet and sat in her seat again.

"Just shake one," he said, "and it gets cold."

For the moment, she set the box aside. "Okay. Can you hoist that foot up here?" She patted her lap.

He bit back a hard groan as he lifted his right foot and cleared the console. Very slowly, he stretched out his leg and gently laid his foot in her lap. He wore lightweight, low-cut hiking shoes.

She pushed up his pant leg. "It's swollen."

"No kidding." He winced as she gently probed at it.

She untied the lace and eased the shoe off and the

low-rise sock as well, dropping them both to the floor beside the first aid kit. "Yep. Swollen. But probably not broken."

"And you know this, how?"

"I don't. But let's think positive, okay? Can you wiggle your toes?"

"Why?"

"I don't know. Don't they always ask if you can do that when you hurt your foot?"

He laughed—a laugh that got caught on a moan. "Some nurse you are." He wiggled his toes. All five of them. "There. What do you think?"

They were very handsome toes, actually, long and well-formed. No weird bumps or bunions.

And what was she thinking? They'd just crashed in the jungle. How good-looking his feet were ought to be the last thing on her mind.

"Zoe?"

"Um, I think I should wrap it and then use the cold packs. And you should keep it elevated."

"Good a suggestion as any."

So she got an ACE bandage from the kit at her feet. She started wrapping at the base of his toes. "Tell me if it's too tight…" She wrapped halfway up his calf and then used the little hooks to secure it. "How's that?"

"Seems fine."

She shook one of the cold packs and it grew icy. Then she used another section of ACE bandage to hold it in place over the swelling. "There. Now we should get you in the back where you can stretch out, get this ankle higher than your heart."

He shook his head. "First, we should see if we can call for help, don't you think?"

"Like…try our cell phones?" That seemed hopeless.

"Let me see about the radio first."

That took about half a minute. The engine—and the radio—were deader than a hammer. They got out their PDAs.

No signal.

He slumped back in his seat, against the door, his leg still canted over to her side, his calf across her knees. "Now it's taped, I might be able to hobble around on it at least. We should try and get to higher ground, somewhere we can build a signal fire." His eyes were drooping as he struggled to stay awake. Maybe she shouldn't have given him two codeines. But at the time, easing his pain had seemed the priority.

"You need to keep that ankle up," she said. "And you're exhausted. You've lost more blood than can possibly be good for you. And you might recall I just sewed up your head? Not right now, Dax. I say we stay in the plane, for the time being anyway. Until the weather clears..." Her words trailed off. The rain had already stopped. And right then, far above their tiny clearing, the sun appeared. Through the water droplets that clung to the side window, everything looked brighter out there.

Well, except for the jungle. It was still a wall of darkest, deepest, scariest green.

Dax said, "Get a pencil. Now." He really was struggling to keep his eyes open.

"Okay, okay..." Her travel purse was on the pilot-side backseat where she'd thrown it while clearing the floor. She reached back and grabbed it, took the pen from the little slot on the side, got the small spiral notebook she always carried from another side pocket. "All right. I'm ready."

He groaned. And then he muttered a latitude and

a longitude. "Those were our coordinates as of right before I brought us down."

She wrote them in her notebook. "You do think of everything."

He didn't answer her. She looked over at him. His eyes were closed, his fine mouth slack.

Good. He needed to rest. And he wasn't going to be doing much of anything when he woke up, not with that ankle. For him, for the next several days, hiking to higher ground was not in the cards. And the signal fire? If she couldn't find a hill very close, she would build it in the clearing.

But not right this minute. For now, they had shelter and a case of bottled water and other clothing when it came to that—and she thought there were blankets in back, too, travel blankets.

She glanced over at Dax again. He was slumped against the other door, his head at a really uncomfortable-looking angle.

Slowly, trying not to hurt his poor ankle any worse, she lifted his foot off her knees. He groaned and tossed his head. She froze. A moment later, with a heavy sigh, he settled down again.

It was a tight fit, but she lowered her seat back and managed to slip out from under him and over the console through the space between the seats. Carefully, she lowered his poor foot to the seat cushion.

Then she put her pen and notebook away and turned for the tangle of suitcases and boxes in the baggage area.

She found a couple of small pillows, the expected travel blankets—and, in a large box bolted to the bulkhead, she found a miracle.

There was toilet paper, paper towels, matches, a

collapsible camping shovel, a couple of dismantled camp chairs she could assemble when the time came. There were two heavy-duty flashlights, a big battery-operated lantern, two oil-burning lanterns with fuel canisters, a small tent, a hatchet…and more. Two cups, two plates. Basic flatware. Two pans for carrying and heating water. There were field glasses and a compass, fishing gear and even a pair of mean-looking hunting knives.

If she could find a stream, she might try fishing. Or maybe she could just jump some jungle creature and stab it with one of the knives. The options, she thought drily, were endless, if somewhat unpleasant.

Right after that, she found several bags of freeze-dried food underneath all the other stuff. Maybe she wouldn't have to go hunting anytime soon after all.

She carried the pillows up in front, eased them under Dax's head and then shook him awake long enough to get him to put his other leg up on her empty seat. She braced the zipped first aid kit, a folded blanket on top, under his bad ankle.

He didn't need a blanket over him. It was plenty warm in the cabin.

For a minute or two, she watched him sleep. He look so good with his shirt off, just as she'd imagined him, with great muscle definition, gorgeous six-pack abs and quite the cute silky-looking happy trail. She didn't begrudge herself a nice, long look. Hey, at this point, anything that took her mind off their desperate situation was a good thing to be doing.

But she couldn't stare at him forever. Reality insisted on intruding. She sat in one of the rear seats, checked her D90, the lenses and the spare camera she'd stored in a suitcase. All had been protected by the padding in their carry cases and were good as new.

That her cameras were okay cheered her somehow. Things could definitely be worse, right?

She started wondering where, exactly, they might have gone down, and considered getting out the paper maps they carried. But later for that. For now, she knew as much as she needed to know: that they were south of the Tropic of Cancer somewhere, in the Mexican jungle. Still in Mexico, because the storm hadn't lasted long enough to blow them *too* far off-course. And even the big fuel capacity of the Cessna 400 wasn't *that* big, not big enough to carry them all the way to Guatemala or Belize.

How long would it be before someone got worried and sent out searchers? They were due to meet Ramón Esquevar for dinner in their beautiful hotel at eight. When they weren't there to meet him maybe? Or even earlier, when they didn't show up at the Tuxtla Gutiérrez airport per their filed flight plan?

She shook her head. Probably not that soon.

Who knew how such things worked?

A small, absurd whimper tried to squeeze out of her throat. She didn't let it. She was strong and whole and smart and she could deal with this. She *would* deal with this.

When Dax woke up, he would *help* her deal with this. Yes, there was the sprained ankle, the gash on his head. But he knew how to survive in a hostile environment. He'd been to a lot of wild places in the world, roughing it, and lived to tell the tale.

What time was it now? Her watch, which seemed to be working fine, said almost four. They didn't do daylight savings in Chiapas, and she'd reset it to San

Cristóbal time when they left Nuevo Laredo. When would dark come? She said a little prayer of thanks for Dax's preparedness. For the box bolted in the bulkhead, with the lanterns and the flashlights and everything else.

When Dax woke up, they would figure out what to do next. Until then, she would simply sit here, safe in the battered plane, and wait.

Except that, all of a sudden, she really, really had to pee.

Which meant she would have to go outside while Dax slept after all.

Hey, at least she had toilet paper.

And a little foray into the clearing wouldn't hurt. She wouldn't go far. She'd take care of business, have a quick look around and duck back inside.

She got the shovel and a roll of paper and set about getting out of the plane, which entailed pushing the back of the passenger seat forward—but not far enough to disturb Dax's propped-up ankle. She held the seat out of the way with one hand and turned the latch to the door with the other.

Wonder of wonders, with only slight resistance, the door went up.

A wall of sticky air came in and wrapped around her—not to mention all the weird jungle sounds: insects buzzing and whirring, birds whose calls she didn't recognize crying in the distance. Rustling noises that instantly brought mental images of scary creatures slithering through the underbrush. She stuck her head out and made the mistake of looking down first.

Only a jagged stump remained where the wing should have been. It must have broken off when the propeller dug in and spun them around like a carnival ride.

Well, all right, then. Even if somehow Dax could manage to get the engine going, they would not be flying out of here in this plane. Yet one more faint hope shattered.

Not that she was going to let negativity take over. She straightened her shoulders and looked around.

Bits of the lost wing littered the area. And without the barrier of the window glass, the jungle only looked darker, denser. If someone was out there, watching from the trees, she would never see them unless they wanted her to.

An image of a group of Zapatista types, in berets and military clothing, armed to the teeth, with great chains of ammo wrapped crossways around their chests, popped into her mind.

But it was only an image. No one emerged to wave an AK-47 at her.

Some small insect buzzed near her ear and she gave it a slap.

Maybe she should put on a shirt.

Another tiny bug attacked. She felt a sting on the side of her neck. She smacked it and then ducked back into the cabin, shutting the door behind her, hauling out her suitcase from the baggage area and grabbing a lightweight shirt with long sleeves and pulling it on. Her legs, in the shorts, would still be vulnerable to bites. But she couldn't cover everything.

There was bug repellent in the back, but her bladder wouldn't wait for that.

Again, she eased the seat forward, swung the door up and tossed the shovel out. Gripping the roll of toilet paper, she dropped down after it, being careful to clear the jagged stub of the wing. The landing gear was gone, too, snapped clean off during the spinning that had ripped away the wing. The belly of the plane rested on the ground. She could easily reach the open door to swing it shut.

For a few seconds, she stood there, swatting at insects, looking around at the small, flat, clear space in the middle of who-knew-where. The tall trees were way, way up there, their wide, thick crowns swaying in a wind that didn't reach the ground. She gazed up, watched a bird sail across the clear blue. It let out a long, fading cry as it went by, a prehistoric sound, the kind the pterodactyls made in *Jurassic Park*. When the ancient cry bled off into nothing, the pressure in her bladder reminded her why she'd come out here in the first place.

No time like the present. She grabbed the shovel and figured out how to extend the handle. There were pegs that popped out along the sides. She stuck the shovel head into the wet ground and hung the paper on a peg.

And then quickly, she took care of business. When that was done, she buried the paper she'd used and then decided on one quick look around before going back inside.

The clearing was a little smaller and narrower than a football field and the plane lay approximately in the center of it. She walked straight out from the passenger door to the edge of the trees, counting off the steps: sixty-five of them. The jungle really was like a wall of living green. She wouldn't try to go in there—not without at least a compass, a knife and the hatchet from that box in the plane.

Instead, she walked the perimeter of the clear space. She found five narrow trails leading off into the undergrowth at various, random-seeming places along the clearing's rim. Made by animals or humans? She had no idea which. All five trails looked well-worn, the thick roots of the trees snaking across them, ready to trip the unwary hiker.

She shivered at the thought that she would probably be going in there, most likely by herself—not yet, though. She would wait until tomorrow morning, when Dax was awake and could advise her on jungle safety. And maybe, if they were very lucky and rescue came quickly, she would never have to go in there at all.

Another of those prehistoric-sounding birds went by overhead. And the cries and rustlings continued from deep in the trees. She went back to the plane and felt only relief to hoist the door and climb to safety within.

Dax was still out cold. And a few of those tiny biting fly-like creatures had joined them inside. She got bug repellent from her suitcase and rubbed it on herself and then on him.

Did he seem too warm? She laid her palm against the side of his face. Maybe a little. But surely not more than a degree or two above normal.

"Water?" he muttered, coming half-awake.

She gave him some. He drank and sank right back into oblivion.

Oh, how she wished she could go there with him. She remembered the bottle of codeine tucked into the first aid kit and thought of taking one herself, of the blessed relief of surrendering to drugged slumber.

She did no such thing. But just the fact that she thought of it brought home, yet again, the deep trouble they were in. She tried to look on the bright side, go over all the things that had actually gone right, beginning with how they weren't dead or critically injured.

How Dax had remembered their location as recently as a minute or two before he tried to land.

The bright side somehow, didn't seem all that bright.

She changed the cold pack on Dax's ankle and then busied herself straightening up the cabin as best she could, gathering the two bloody shirts, stuffing them in an old canvas tote she'd brought along. Maybe later she could wash them, if she could find a stream. They would never be white again, but in the jungle, who was going to care? If nothing else, they would do as cloths for washing, for drying their few dishes and cups.

In the box with the camping gear, she found flares. They would be at least as good as a signal fire, should a plane go by overhead. She took them out and put them on the floor of the rear seat, close at hand.

It had been hours since she'd eaten—since her early breakfast of a protein drink and toast. Her stomach seemed to have shut down, probably some natural reaction to the shock of what had happened.

But she knew that she needed to eat to keep up her strength. So she got a bag of freeze-dried beef stew and poured some water in it. It was not delicious. She gagged it down anyway and found she felt marginally better afterward, stronger.

Dax should probably try to eat something, too. She found a bag of maple sugar oatmeal, added water and tried to feed it to him. He woke up, ate a few bites, and then mumbled, "No. No more…water?"

She gave him some. He went back to sleep and she ate the rest of the oatmeal so it wouldn't go to waste.

Outside, it was still daylight, would be for at least a couple of hours. She had some books on her laptop, but it seemed somehow foolish to start wearing down the battery. So she got out the paper maps that were required for small-plane travel, and her pen and notebook and marked the coordinates Dax had given her.

She learned that they were in the Chiapan wilderness, miles and miles north of San Cristóbal. She stared at the small dot she'd made on the map for a long time, as if just by looking at it, she could figure out how to get them out of here.

No magic realization as to escape came to her. She yawned and leaned her head against the seat and thought wearily that at last the adrenaline from all this excitement was wearing off. Even shaky, scared crash victims get tired eventually.

She got up and changed the cold pack on Dax's ankle again. He didn't stir and seemed to be sleeping peacefully.

Then, since she could think of nothing else that needed doing right that instant, she put the rear seat as far back as it would go and closed her eyes.

Her sleep was fitful. She dreamed of a party in a big, rambling house. She roamed from room to room. Everyone was having a great time and she didn't know anyone there.

And then she started dreaming that she was at work, at *Great Escapes*. No one was there. The place was empty. But then she heard Dax. He was moaning, calling out, saying strange, garbled, things. Words she didn't understand, nonsense syllables.

In her dream, she looked for him. She called to him, but couldn't find him.

Slowly, she woke and realized where she was, lost in the Chiapan jungle somewhere, in a wrecked plane. And Dax was in the front seat, tossing around, moaning.

It was dark out. She got the battery-run lantern from

the box in back. Switching it on, she craned over the seats and Dax's agitated form. She set the lantern on the floor in front. The powerful beam, focused on the ceiling, gave plenty of weirdly slanted, glaring light.

She bent over Dax. He was moaning, tossing his head, scrunched down at a neck-breaking angle against the pilot-side door.

He mumbled to himself, "No…tired…cold…hot…" And then a flood of nonsense words. He shivered, violently.

And he was sweating—his face and chest were shiny wet. She was glad she'd wrapped the bandage around his head. If she'd settled for taping it on, so much sweat would likely have loosened it. She reached over the seat to try to ease him back up onto the pillows.

The heat of his skin shocked her. He was burning up.

Chapter Six

Dax was a little boy again. His mother was gone. She had been gone for a whole year now.

She had "passed on," his Nanny Ellen said. Jesus had taken her to be with the angels.

Dax thought that was very mean of Jesus. The angels didn't need a mother. Not like a little boy did. The angels were beautiful and they could fly. They wore white dresses and had long, gold hair.

His father got angry when he heard what Nanny Ellen said about his mother going to the angels. His dad said Nanny shouldn't fill the boy's head with silly superstition—and then he got his briefcase and went to work.

Dax's dad was always working. Always gone. Dax had Nanny Ellen and he liked the stories Nanny told, about the angels, about the loaves and fish that were always enough to feed the hungry people, no matter how many of them there were. He liked Nanny Ellen.

But he liked his dad more. He *loved* his dad. Someday he would be all grown-up. He would go to work like his dad and his dad would talk to him because he would be a man, a man who worked, not a little boy who wanted his dad with him and missed his mother.

There was a hand on his cheek, a gentle hand. The hand slipped around and cradled his head. A woman's voice said, "Shh, now. It's okay. You're going to get better, Dax. Drink this…"

He opened his eyes. Slowly, a woman's face came into focus, a tired face, but a beautiful one. The woman had red hair and the bluest eyes.

He thought that he wanted to kiss her, to touch the soft skin of her cheek. If only he weren't so worn out.

So weak.

He remembered, then. He was a man now. And his dad was dead, too, as dead as his mom. And there had been something…something that had happened.

Something that was all his fault.

Wait.

Now he remembered. He knew what he'd done. They were supposed to fly commercial. She'd had it all set up. But he had insisted that *he* would fly them.

And he had. Right into the jungle. Right into the ground.

He drank from the cup she put to his lips. It was warm, what she gave him. A warm broth. And that surprised him. They were somewhere deep in the jungle, after all, with no stove or microwave in sight. He said the word, "Warm…"

She smiled at him, a smile as beautiful as those

of any of Nanny Ellen's angels. "I built a fire, in the clearing. I've managed to keep it going."

He sipped a little more, swallowed, "How long…?" His voice trailed off. Words were hard to come by. His throat felt dust-bowl dry.

She finished for him. "….have we been here?"

At his nod, she told him, "This is the fourth day."

The fourth day? How could that be possible? He whispered, wonderingly, "So much time…"

"You've been very sick. Drink a little more."

He obeyed her. It felt good, the warmth, going down. He realized he was stretched across the backseat. Hadn't he been in the front before? He asked, "Back…seat?"

She nodded. "I managed to get you back here the second day. You don't remember?"

"No. Nothing…"

"It's better for you back here, without that big console between the seats."

Outside, lightning flashed. The answering clap of thunder seemed very close. Hard rain pounded the plane.

"Rescue?" he asked.

Her smile was tender. "Not yet."

His eyes were so heavy. He wanted to stay awake, to talk to her, to find out all that had happened, to make sure she was okay, that nothing had hurt her because of his foolish need to buy big toys and then take risks with them. But his eyes would not obey the commands of his brain.

He couldn't keep them open any longer. "Zoe. Thank you, Zoe…"

"Shh. Sleep now. Your fever's broken and you are going to get better. Just rest. Just sleep."

He dreamed of Nora—Nora, crying. Nora begging him to understand.

"Please, Dax. I know when we got married I said I was willing to wait. But I'm pregnant now and we are going to have to make the best of it."

"Liar," he said to her, low and deadly. He said all the rotten things, the cruel things he had said all those years ago. He accused her. He'd always known how much she wanted a baby. And he didn't believe in accidents.

"I'm so sorry." The words were a plea for his acceptance, his forgiveness. She swore to him that it *had* been an accident, her big brown eyes flooded with guilty tears, her soft red mouth trembling.

He wasn't ready. He didn't know if he would ever be ready.

But he knew it wasn't right, to be so cruel to her. He was going to be a father. He needed to start learning to accept that.

So in the end, he reached for her, he wrapped his arms around her and held her close. He comforted her. He dried her tears. He said it would be all right.

"All right, Nora. We'll work it out. It's all right…."

A cool cloth bathed his face, his neck. "Shh, now. Shh…"

He opened his eyes, half expecting to see his ex-wife gazing down at him. But it wasn't Nora. "Zoe."

"I was just going to check your bandage."

"Is it…?" He reached up to touch his forehead.

She caught his hand, guided it back down. "It's fine. Healing well."

He blinked away the last of the dream about Nora. "What day?"

"It's Friday."

"The fifth day…"

"Yep."

"No rescue plane, no search party…"

She slowly shook her head. "By now, it's safe to assume they have been looking. By now, my father knows. He will have mobilized and when my father mobilizes, things get done. But no sign of anyone looking for us so far. I found the flares from that large, wonderful, lifesaving box of equipment of yours and I haven't had a chance to use one yet."

Five days, he thought. And how much longer would they have to last here? Were they going to die here? He said, "It's a big jungle."

"But you gave me the coordinates, remember? We know approximately where we are. Eventually, we can try and walk out of here if we have to."

He said what he was thinking. "But we shouldn't have to. We should be wrapping up our 'great escape' in San Cristóbal de las Casas about now. And we would be, except for the fact that I'm a fatheaded ass who had to show off his pretty little plane."

"Stop that," she said sharply. "Don't you even go there, Dax Girard. This plane was perfectly safe. The weather was the problem."

"But if I had only listened to you—"

"If, if, if. Please. You want to talk if? Fine. What about if I hadn't proposed this trip in the first place, what if you hadn't liked the idea? And we can always go in the other direction. What if you weren't an excellent pilot? What if you hadn't had the foresight to install that box full of necessary equipment in the back? What if you hadn't put together a first aid kit that has everything but an operating table inside? We cannot afford to get all up into the 'if' game, Dax. We need to keep our chins up and our minds focused on what needs doing next."

He stared up at her. "Wow," he said.

"Wow, what?" She glared down at him.

He didn't even try to hide the admiration he knew had to be written all over his face. "I don't think I realized until now just how tough you are."

"I have seven bossy brothers and a pigheaded dad. You're damn right I'm tough."

His stomach chose that moment to growl. He put his hand on it. "I think I'm starving."

Her sudden grin was like the sun coming up. "And that is a very good sign."

The next day, which was Saturday, she helped him get up on his feet and out of the plane for the first time since they'd left Nuevo Laredo almost a week before. Every muscle, every bone, every inch of his skin—all of it ached. He was weak as a newborn baby. And he was filthy. He could smell himself and the smell was not a good one.

But his ankle was healing faster than even he could have hoped. He could put weight on it, gingerly, could hobble around if he took his time and was careful. Zoe had a camp set up, with the two collapsible camp chairs from the box in the baggage area, the tent and the few cooking utensils. And a campfire ringed by rocks she had gathered, with a large, jagged piece of the wing nearby. It took him a moment to understand the purpose of the piece of wing.

Then it came to him. When it rained, she could use it to shield the fire a little, to keep at least some of the coals dry. The wood she'd collected waited under another hunk of the ruined plane.

She had water heating for him.

He shaved. In the small mirror from his travel kit, his face looked haggard, pale and drawn. Beneath the fresh dressing she'd put on his head wound, his eyes stared back at him, sunken and haunted.

"I look like hell," he told her.

She poked at the fire and nodded. "Yes, you do. Hurry up. I have a surprise."

He wished for the impossible. "A shower would be nice."

"Close. You'll see. Finish your shave."

Something close to a shower. That, he wanted. He wanted it bad and he wanted it now. He shaved faster, nicking himself twice and hardly caring.

When his face was smooth again and he'd put his kit away, she got him some clean clothes. She gave him one of the hunting knives, one of the two canteens and a bottle of shampoo.

"I need a knife to take a shower?" he asked.

"You never know what you might need once you get in the trees," she warned.

"We're going into the trees?" It was a stupid question. Of course they were going into the trees. He could see the whole clearing by turning in a circle. There was nothing that would provide anything resembling a shower anywhere in it. But how far would they be going? He couldn't make it any distance on his weak ankle.

"Not far," she said, as if she'd read his mind. "And I'll help you. We'll take it slow." One of the travel blankets was strung on a line she'd run between the plane and the camping shovel. She grabbed that and slung it around her neck, stuck the other hunting knife in a loop of her waistband along with the other canteen, and grabbed the hatchet she had found in the equipment box. "Come on, wrap your arm across my shoulders."

He obeyed. Together, they hobbled toward the forest.

The trail became clear as they approached it. They went in, the trees closing around them, into deep shadow. Without a breeze. Instantly, the insects started biting.

"Ignore them," she said. "It's not far." She led him onward. He focused on hopping along, trying not to trip on the thick ropes of exposed roots that twined across the trail.

Maybe fifty yards in, with the clearing just a memory somewhere behind them, she stopped. "Listen. You hear it?"

He did. A hard, hollow rushing sound. He probably shouldn't have been surprised. Rivers were everywhere in the jungle. Still, he felt excitement rising. "A river?" Rivers not only meant a place to wash away the filth and maybe even catch some fish to eat, they were the highways of the wilderness. You followed them and eventually, you found people—people who might help you to make your way home.

She nodded. She looked very pleased with herself. "Yes, a river. Come on, it's not far now."

And it wasn't. Another ten yards or so and the trail opened up and there it was, gleaming in the sun that shone down through the gap in the trees. They stood on the bank and he admired the gorgeous sight. There was a waterfall above, a nice inviting pool below, right in front of them. Some distance to his left, the shallows formed rapids that raced away downstream.

"Have you tried fishing yet?" he asked.

She shook her head. "The freeze-dried stuff isn't

going to last forever, though. We need to get out that pole. I would have done it sooner..."

Guilt, ever-present since the crash, pricked him again. "But you were afraid to leave me alone for that long."

"Well, there's that. Plus, I've always hated fishing. I don't have the patience for it, which is probably why I never catch anything."

At last. Something she actually might need him for. "I'll do it, no problem. Best to try at dusk, though, when the fish are biting."

"I was really hoping you would volunteer for it—but what about bait?"

"I'm guessing we can find some worms or a grub or two."

She wrinkled her nose, which was red and peeling a little, but nonetheless as good to look at as the rest of her. "You get to bait the hook *and* catch the fish."

"It would be my pleasure."

They shared a long glance, a glance that said a lot of things neither of them was willing to speak aloud.

"Well?" she demanded at last. "You coming in or not?" She ducked out from under his arm and he steadied himself with his weight on his good foot.

She dropped the hatchet and blanket to the sun-warmed jut of rock they stood on and shoved down her shorts, kicked off her shoes and removed her shirt. Beneath, she wore a red two-piece swimsuit. Her normally pale skin had a ruddy cast now, from the past six days in the clearing, where the sun shone bright between the sudden fierce rainstorms. Her red hair fell past her shoulders, gleaming, and her slim body curved softly in all the right places.

She wasn't wearing that ridiculous fake diamond. Come to think of it, he hadn't seen it since the crash.

He watched her adjust the straps of the red top and he felt desire rising. To touch her, to hold her, to learn all the secrets of her pretty, slender body. He really must be getting well.

Back off, Dax, the voice of wisdom within advised.

He heeded that voice. He would not touch her. Or hold her. They understood each other. She worked for him and in the end, it was a lot harder to find a top-notch assistant than a bed partner. Any willing woman could give him sex.

Zoe had a thousand other talents, useful talents. If they made it back, he intended to find ways to keep her working for him for a very long time.

If...

Her heated words of the day before came to him. *We can't afford to get all up in the "if" game, Dax.* She was right about that—as she was about a lot of things.

He put all the nagging doubts as to the likelihood of their survival from his mind and he focused on the moment, as it was, free of expectation, sexual or otherwise. On the pretty woman in the red swimsuit, on the clear pool and the dazzling, roaring waterfall, waiting for him in the sun.

Zoe laughed as she waded in. "Watch out for the crocodiles."

He thought she was kidding—but then he saw the long, knobby narrow head gliding through the water near the opposite bank. "There's one over there." He pointed.

She laughed again and started splashing. The crocodile turned and went the other way. "They're shy," she said. "I remember reading that somewhere. Not like their Asian relatives at all. And I've discovered since we've been here that it's true—but that doesn't mean I didn't scream bloody murder the first time I saw that big guy over there."

Awkwardly, he lowered himself to the rock. He took off his shoes and socks and unwound the bandage that supported his ankle. It was still a little puffy, but nowhere near as bad as it had been before.

He pulled his shirt over his head and got out of his khaki shorts. In only his boxer briefs and the bandage on his forehead, he struggled upright again. With the bottle of shampoo in his hand, he limped into the water.

It felt wonderful. Cool, clean. Fresh. And as soon as he got in as far as his waist, his injured ankle stopped hobbling him. Keeping his head above water in order not to get his bandage wet, he swam around a little, just because it felt so good.

And then he moved closer to the bank again, got to where he could stand up, and waded to waist deep. He squirted some shampoo on his palm. It smelled of tropical flowers. *Plumeria*, according to the label, which showed a woman bathing in a tub full of pink blooms.

Not a manly scent, but so what? It had soap in it and it would get him clean.

Zoe swam to him, her hair streaming out behind her, a banner of wet silk, the color of fire. "Here. I'll hold the bottle."

He handed it over and then used the shampoo to wash himself, ducking down up to his neck to rinse off the lather when he was done.

She said, "Be careful. I don't want you getting that bandage wet."

"Then you'd better wash my hair for me." He moved up the bank a couple more steps, until he could get on his knees and still have his shoulders above the water. "Go for it."

She took a small puddle of the shampoo in her hand and gave him back the bottle. Then she circled around behind him and went to work.

Her hands were careful, firm and knowing. "Tip your head back."

He did, and he closed his eyes as she shampooed him, working up a lather, massaging his scalp in a thoroughly pleasurable way. It was good, to have her hands on him. Almost as if his flesh had memorized her touch, through the days he was so sick, when she tended him so carefully—and constantly. As if his skin had learned the feel of hers by heart, and now craved the contact it no longer received.

He wondered if she might be feeling anything similar. Proprietary, maybe? She had been all he had for five days, his comfort, his only hope of survival. She had, in a sense, owned him, had done whatever was needed, no matter how intimate or unpleasant, to keep him alive, to help him fight the fever that tried to claim him. She had fed him, cleaned him up as best she could, changed his bandages and his clothes.

His memories of that time were indistinct. Mostly he had lived in a fevered dream. But he remembered her touch, soothing him, comforting him. More than once, when the chills racked him, she had lain down with him, wrapped her own body around him, to soothe him, to keep him warm.

"Feels good," he said, his tone huskier than he should have allowed it to be.

She washed his ears, her fingers sliding along the

curves and ridges, meticulous and tender. Cradling his head with her fingers, she used her thumbs against his scalp, rubbing in circles. He almost groaned in pleasure when she did that, but swallowed the sound just in time.

"All right," she said, too soon. "Let your legs float up."

He did. She cradled his head in the water with one hand and carefully rinsed away the lather with the other.

"Okay. All finished."

He wanted to stay right where he was, floating face up with his eyes shut to block out the glare of the sun, her hand in his hair, supporting him, for at least another week or so. But obediently, he lowered his feet to the sandy river bottom and backed away from her. "Thanks."

She sent him a quick smile and moved closer to shore where she could toss the shampoo up onto the rock with the rest of their things.

They swam for a while, laughing, happy as little kids in their own private pool. She led him under the falls and they crouched on a big rock inside and stared through the veil of roaring water at the indistinct, shimmering world beyond.

"You ought to get your camera in here," he suggested.

She nodded. "I've thought about it. But I didn't bring one that's waterproof."

"Get any other good shots?"

"A few. I have to be careful, not go shutter crazy. I want to make the battery charge last as long as I can."

And how long would it be, until she could recharge her cameras? The question—and others like it—was never far from his mind. Or hers either, judging by the way she looked at him, and then quickly glanced away.

How long until someone found them? How long until his ankle healed and he could lead them out of here?

"Don't," she whispered gently.

He didn't have to ask, *Don't what?* He only gave her a curt nod and slid back into the water and under the falls.

They got out onto the rocks eventually, and dried themselves in the sun. She stretched out on the blanket she'd brought. He limped along the shoreline, looking for a good walking stick.

Found one, too. He figured with it, he could get back to camp without having to lean on her the whole way.

Before they returned to the clearing, they gathered firewood to take with them and filled the two canteens. She explained that she would boil the water, just to be on the safe side. She'd saved the empty water bottles and she was refilling them with the sterilized river water.

He marveled at her resourcefulness. She'd probably be halfway to San Cristóbal by now, living off the land, if not for his holding her back.

She sent him a look. "I can read your mind, you know."

"Okay. Now you're scaring me."

"It's your nature to be fatheaded and overly sure of yourself. Just go with your nature. No dragging around being morose, okay?"

He laughed then, because she was right. There was a bright side and he would look on it. They were both alive and surviving pretty damn effectively, thanks to her.

"It can only get better from here," he said.

"That's the spirit." She hooked her canteen on her belt, pulled a couple of lengths of twine from her pocket and handed him one. "Tie up your firewood."

He did what she told him to do—just as he'd been doing for most of the day. After the wood was bundled, they gathered up the stuff they had left on the rock and headed for the trail.

Back at camp, he propped his ankle up to rest it. They ate more of the dwindling supply of freeze-dried food and pored over the maps.

She had marked the location he'd made her write down the night of the crash. It appeared that their own personal jungle was somewhere in the northernmost tip of the state of Chiapas, about a hundred and twenty-five miles from the state capital of Tuxtla Gutiérrez and the airport where they were supposed to have landed. There were any number of tiny villages and towns in northern Chiapas, and deforested farmland and ranches were supposed to cover most of the area where they had gone down.

Actually, he calculated that they shouldn't *be* in rainforest, but they were. And that meant that they must have been blown farther south after he noted the coordinates that final time. And *that* meant who the hell knew where they were? Their best bet remained to follow the river until they found human habitation.

And when would they be doing that?

At least a week, maybe two, depending on how fast his ankle healed.

That evening, as the sun dipped low, they slathered themselves in bug repellent and returned to the river with the fishing pole and a plastic bag containing grubs he had found under rocks at the edge of the clearing.

He assembled his pole and baited his line while she gathered more wood and tied it into twin bundles and then sat down with him to wait with him for the fish to bite.

They didn't have to wait long. He felt the first stirrings of renewed self-respect when he recognized the sharp tug on the line.

"Got one." He played the line, letting it spin out and then reeling it in. Finally, he hauled the fish free of the water. It was a beautiful sight, the scaly body twisting and turning, gleaming in the fading light, sending jewel-like drops of water flying in a wide arc.

Zoe laughed and clapped her hands and shot her fist in the air. "Way to go, Girard! That baby's big enough to make dinner for both of us."

He caught the squirming fish in his hand and eased out the hook. "You know how to clean them?"

She groaned. "Unfortunately, yes." She did the messy job while he baited his hook again.

He landed another one, just because he could. The meat would probably stay fresh enough for their morning meal. They could try smoking them to preserve them, and they would. Tomorrow. For tonight, two was more than enough. He cleaned that second fish himself, found a stick to hang them on and they started back.

Zoe took the lead with the two bundles of firewood and a full canteen. Dax, leaning on his cane, carrying the fish and his pole, followed behind.

They were almost to the clearing when the giant snake dropped out of the trees and landed on Zoe.

Chapter Seven

It was almost fully dark by then. In the trees, it was hard to see your hand in front of your face, so it took Dax a few seconds to make out what was happening.

Zoe let out a blood-curdling shriek and then one word, "Snake!"

He made out the thick, twisting form, the white belly gleaming, coiling itself around her as she sent the firewood flying. Dax dropped the stick with the fish on it, tossed his cane and pole to the trail and whipped out his hunting knife.

By then, she had managed to turn and face him. The snake started hissing, a loud, ugly sound. "Here," she said, her voice straining as she tried to control the powerful coils. He realized she had a hold of the neck, right below the extremely large head, in both hands. "Cut here…"

He stepped up, grabbed the snake a foot below her

clutching fists and sliced that sucker's head clean off. Blood spurted and the thunderous hissing stopped. He felt the spray on his face. The snake's powerful tail whipped at him, strongly at first and then more slowly.

Zoe held on to the detached head, whimpering, muttering to herself, "Eeuuu, icky, sticky. Yuck!" as he dropped the long, thick scaly body and it gradually went limp.

It shocked the hell out of him, to watch her lose it. Up till then, she'd been a model of determined cool and unbreakable self-control. "Zoe…"

"Oh, God. God help us. Oh, ick. Oh, help…."

He gaped at her, disbelieving. And then he shook himself. She needed talking down and she needed it now. And he was the only one there to do it. He spoke softly, slowly, "It's okay, Zoe. It's okay. It's dead."

She went on whimpering, muttering nonsense words, clutching the severed head of the reptile, as though she feared if she let it go, it would snap back to life and attack her all over again.

"Zoe. Zoe, come on. Let go." He caught her wrists in his hands. "It's dead. It can't hurt you anymore. You can let go."

With a wordless cry, she threw the snake's head down and hurled herself at his chest.

He tottered a little on his bad ankle but recovered, steadied himself and wrapped his arms around her. Gathering her good and close, he stroked her hair, whispering, "Okay, it's okay…"

She buried her face against his shoulder, and huddled against him, trembling. "I was so scared. So damn scared…"

He kissed the top of her head without even stopping

to think that maybe he was crossing the line. Right then, there was no line. Only her need to be held—and his, to hold her. "I know, I know. But it's over now."

"You're right. Over. It's over, it's okay…" Slowly, she quieted. The shaking stopped. She lifted her head and looked up at him. He saw the gleam of her eyes through the gloom.

He wondered if she'd been bitten. The snake was a boa, he was reasonably sure. Their bites weren't deadly, but they could hurt like hell. He asked, carefully, "Were you bitten?"

She shook her head. "No. Uh-uh. It just, it was so strong, slithering around me, tightening…."

He felt her shudder and hurried to remind her, "But it's dead now." He spoke firmly, "Dead."

"Dead. Yes." She nodded, a frantic bobbing of her head. And then she blinked. "Do you know how many times I walked this path while you were so sick?"

He captured her sweet face between his hands, held her gaze and didn't let his waver. "Don't. No *what-ifs,* remember?"

"But I—"

He tipped her chin higher, made her keep looking at him. "No. Don't go there. You're safe and we won't go to the river, or even into the trees, except together from now on. If one of us is in danger, the other will be there, to help deal with it."

"Oh, Dax…"

He didn't think, didn't stop to consider that he wasn't supposed to put any moves on her, that she had great value to him and they had certain agreements, the main one being hands off.

It just seemed the most natural thing to do. The right thing.

The only thing.

He lowered his head and she lifted hers.

They met in the middle. He tasted her mouth, so soft, still trembling, so warm and needful—needing *him*. She sighed and her breath was his breath.

He wrapped her closer, slanted his head the other way, deepened the amazing, impossible kiss.

Our first kiss...

A miracle. Of heat and tender, yearning flesh, of wonder.

He pressed her to open. She did and he tasted her, his tongue in her mouth, against her teeth, and her tongue in his, gliding on top, touching the roof of his mouth, as if to taste all of him, to know him, all of him.

In every way.

Our first kiss...

It went on and on. Delicious. Hungry. Beautiful. They stood there, wrapped tight together, in the dark jungle, the big snake limp around their feet, and they kissed and kissed some more.

Finally, with a last, reluctant sigh, she pulled away and lifted her eyes to him. She looked strangely dazed and her lips were shiny, slightly swollen. "We should... the river. Go back. I need to wash away the blood." They were both breathing hard, as if they'd just run a long race.

He nodded down at her. "Yeah. All right. Of course."

They stared at each other, shared a look as hungry, as seeking and endless as the kiss had been. And then she stepped back. He let his arms drop away, releasing her.

By some radar between them, some tacit agree-ment, neither of them mentioned the line they had just crossed, the forbidden terrain they had let themselves stumble into.

She waited for him to turn, to lead the way back to the water.

He said, "We can leave the wood here. But nothing else." Any meat could be gone before they returned, carried off by scavengers. "Take the fish."

She bent down and picked up the stick with the two fish dangling from it. He got his knife from where he'd dropped it, wiped it on his pant leg and returned it to its sheath. He felt around among the twisting roots that crisscrossed the trail until he found the pole and his walking stick.

And then he picked up the snake and wrapped it around his neck.

She gasped. "Wh—what are you doing?"

"It's meat, Zoe. It's protein." He found the severed head, tossed it into the trees.

"Ugh."

He arched a brow, suggested hopefully, "Tastes like chicken."

"Ugh," she said again. But she didn't argue. "Can we go?"

"After you." He wobbled upright and moved aside, settling the dead reptile more comfortably around his neck. The damn thing had to be eight feet long.

She slipped around him soundlessly, giving him as wide a berth as possible on the narrow trail, and headed back the way they'd come.

He caught her arm when they reached the pool. "Don't go in."

She turned and looked at him, a watchful look, and then carefully freed herself from his grip. "Because?"

"There could be piranhas."

She made a scoffing sound. It reassured him, to see her confident, take-charge nature reasserting itself. "If there were, don't you think we would know by now?"

"They attack when there's blood in the water."

The nearly full moon shone down on them now. He could see her pretty face clearly. The snake's blood on her cheek looked black in the moonlight. "Ah." And she nodded. "Okay."

So she set the fish aside and crouched on the rock to scoop water into her palms and scrub at her cheeks, her arms and neck. He washed, too, awkwardly, with only one good ankle to support his crouching weight, the other leg stretched out and aching a little, growing tired from all the activity that day.

They rose without speaking. She took up the fish. He hung the snake around his neck again, grabbed his pole and his walking stick. They headed, once more, into the trees.

The fish was good.

The snake meat was better.

They ate their fill. He felt stronger almost instantly, his body grateful for the much-needed protein.

After the meal, she changed the bandage on his forehead. Then, with his bad leg propped and resting, he cut the rest of the snake meat into strips. Since they both agreed he should try and stay off his weak ankle, he had Zoe dig a pit close to the plane and then shovel in hot coals from the campfire. At his instruction, she got a canvas poncho from his suitcase and the spare campfire rack from the bottom of the box in the baggage area.

She slanted him a look when she brought out the

rack. "I can't believe you thought to store these racks in there."

He shrugged. "If you cook over a campfire, you need something to put the meat on."

She did the rest, following his instructions, laying out the meat so the smoke would cure it, keeping the fire low. The poncho went on top, positioned with just enough ventilation to make it nice and smoky inside.

He had her find another piece of wing to lean against the fuselage, thus protecting the pit from the afternoon rains. They would have to check the fire in there regularly, keep it going, but not too high.

"How long will it take?" she asked.

"A couple of days. The dried meat will be good for about a week. When the snake is cured, we can smoke fish, too—though with the river nearby, I don't really think we need to."

She dropped into the chair beside him. "You're very convenient to have around."

"Back at ya, and then some." They shared one of those looks that said everything they couldn't quite say aloud.

It was getting late by then. The moon rode high over the clearing and the fire kept the bugs at bay. For a while, neither of them spoke. He was avoiding climbing back into the plane and trying to sleep in the backseat that had been his sickbed. Would she sleep in the tent? He didn't remember where she'd slept those first few nights, but last night she'd left him and taken the tent.

She was looking at him again.

He met her watchful gaze. "What?"

"We might never get back to SA, you know."

"We will." As he said the words, he realized he

believed them. "And didn't we agree not to play the *what-if* game?"

She waved a hand. "That was when you were blaming yourself. This is...well, you know, just getting real."

"We'll get back. That's real."

"And you know this, how?"

"We might have both been born of money, grown up having it easy, but that doesn't make us any less tough and smart. We're survivors. We have tools, the right clothing, decent footwear. And in terms of abundant food sources, getting stranded in the jungle is not a bad choice. If nobody comes to find us, when my ankle is healed enough, we're going to walk out of here. Our chances are good. Better than good."

She studied his face. He wondered what she was seeking. "If—*when* we get back, I want my job, Dax."

He swore low. "Come on. I may be fatheaded and overbearing, but I know quality help when I have it. Did I say something to make you think I wasn't aware of your value to me and to *Great Escapes?*"

"You kissed me."

So that was it. "A lapse. I apologize."

"Why apologize? I kissed you back." She licked her lips, as if the taste of him lingered. "And I liked it when you kissed me. I liked it a lot."

So much frankness made his breath catch and heat pool in his groin. He said, rough and low, "We have an understanding. I've been trying to abide by it. You're not helping me to keep it, when you talk like this, when you look at me that way."

She refused to look away. "It's so simple now, here. I see everything through a lens of that simplicity, of the need to survive. I see that there are a thousand ways to die here. I see that we're something else to each other, here. Something important. We are each other's survival, each other's lifeline. And if you're wrong and I do die here, I don't want to die regretting the fact that I never made love with you."

He clutched the aluminum arms of the chair to keep from reaching for her and he said, with careful coolness, "I feel the same. But it's okay. You're *not* going to die. I thought I just explained that."

She smiled. How could a smile be that sad and at the same time that full of primal knowledge? And then she broke the searing gaze they shared and stared into the fire. After a minute, in a voice barely above a whisper, she spoke again, "I used to think you were trying purposely to tempt me."

"Yeah, well. You thought right. And you never gave in, were never anything but beautiful and charming, quick with the comebacks—and strictly professional."

"We could make another agreement…for now, while we're here in this wild place and it's just you and me, surviving, taking what joy we can any way we can find it."

His mouth was dry. He gripped the chair arms all the harder. "What agreement?"

"We change the rules, for now, just for as long as we're here, in the jungle. And when we get home, I get my job back and we become strictly professional with each other again."

Yes. The affirmative was there, on the tip of his tongue. It was an urgent need in him to say whatever she wanted him to say, so that he could have her and have her now. He managed, somehow, not to let that *yes* out. "You really think that's possible, to go back? In my experience, it never works."

"I intend to make it work. I *will* make it work."

He found that he believed her, as he believed they would get back to San Antonio. She was an extraordinary woman and if she said she could do a thing, who was he, a mere man, to doubt her? "I'm not going to be able to keep arguing about this, Zoe. I don't *want* to argue. I want to get in that tent with you and kiss every inch of you."

Her mouth trembled. And her eyes were dark right then, dark and as full of secrets as the night itself. "So don't argue."

"I have one more question."

"Ask."

"Johnny?"

She laughed, then, a low, throaty, knowing sound. "There is no Johnny."

"I knew it."

"I knew you knew. And now *I* have a question."

"Name it."

"Did you bring condoms with you?"

"I always have condoms with me."

She almost smiled at that—but not quite. "Well, all right, then." She swept upward, out of the chair, and stood above him, holding down her hand.

He looked up at her and knew he would never forget the sight of her at that moment, of her red hair haloed in firelight, her blue eyes shadowed, full of hot promises that he fully intended to make her keep.

Still, he couldn't stop himself from asking one more time, "You're sure?"

"Take my hand, Dax. Let's go to bed."

Chapter Eight

Zoe didn't doubt herself, didn't second-guess. The course was set. She would follow it.

She would glory in it.

When he reached up his lean hand to her, she took it, grasped it tight, helped pull him up, helped steady him on his good foot. He touched her face with his other hand, traced her brows, followed the curve of her cheek.

And then he kissed her.

It was a slow, tender, exploratory kiss. She lifted her mouth to him and let him take the lead, drinking in the scent of him: clean sweat, insect repellent—and a hint of plumeria from her shampoo. And something else, something heady and manly and totally wonderful. Something that was every good smell in the world, all rolled into one. A one-of-a-kind scent that almost had her believing in those "special" pheromones of his that

Lin was always going on about. He smelled of chocolate and sugar cookies fresh from the oven. Of toasted pecans. Oh, she definitely wanted to eat him right up.

He ran his tongue along the seam where her lips met and she let him in.

That was when he wrapped his big arms around her and pulled her close to his hard, strong chest. The fire bathed them in its red glow, sending up sparks to the velvety night. Off in the darkness, she heard the jungle sounds, the screams of predators, the calls of nightbirds, the endless rustling of creatures that crept close to the ground.

She smiled against his mouth, eased her hands around his tight waist, reveled in the feel of him, pressed so close with passionate intent. At last.

In time, he lifted his head and looked down at her through those glorious, lazy bedroom eyes.

She said, "When you were so sick, when you were shaking with fever, shivering with cold at the same time, I used to lie down with you."

"I remember. I was so grateful. Comforted."

"It was a comfort to me, too—and a tight fit on those seats."

A smile tipped on a corner of his beautiful mouth. "But you made it work."

"Hmm." She lifted on tiptoe.

He took the hint and lowered his head to her again.

She claimed his lips eagerly, hungrily. When he held her and kissed her, it all made sense, somehow. That they were here, miles from home, constantly in danger but together.

In every way.

For a long while, they simply stood there by the fire, kissing, whispering to each other, kissing some more.

Yes, she felt an urgency to take the pleasure farther, faster. She sensed that he did, too.

But there was a certain joy, a delicious thrill, in denying the urgency, in taking their time.

His hardness pressed into her belly, making promises that they both knew would be kept, and kept that night. Her body thrummed with excitement, her breasts ached for his caress. And below, she was heavy. Liquid with yearning, with hot expectation.

And they went on kissing even longer.

In time, he released her. They didn't need words. She banked the fire. They each made a final trip into the shadows. They washed their hands and faces, brushed their teeth. He got the condoms from a suitcase and she collected the blanket and pillow that remained in the plane.

And then, at last, they entered the tent.

He undressed her first. Each time she tried to get something of his off, he gently pushed her eager hands away.

And eventually, she surrendered. After days of always having to be in control and on guard, it was a revelation, a sweet and voluptuous relief, to lie back on the pillows. To let him bring pleasure to her.

Like the kissing by the fire, he took his time about it. Starting with her shoes and socks, he worked his way up her body, kissing and caressing as he peeled away her clothing, revealing all her secrets.

She was only too happy to be revealed. It was exactly what she wanted, and just the way she wanted it. His tongue was magic, his fingers knew the perfect way to touch her. To stroke her.

Halfway up her body, he lingered. She still had

on her shirt and bra when he dipped his tongue into the well of her navel, when he kissed every inch of her belly.

And lower.

He touched the chestnut curls and she opened her legs for him. He whispered how beautiful she was, how much he wanted her, how the taste of her was so sweet, even better than he had dreamed in his constant fantasies of her.

"Constant?" That sounded really good.

"Yes. As in continuous. As in you've made me crazy..."

"Crazy. Good. That's very good."

A low chuckle rumbled in his chest. "I knew you'd think so." He lowered his head to her, his fingers gently parting her secret flesh. "So beautiful. So slick and hot and wet..." And then his mouth was there, doing things. Wonderful things.

She groaned and clutched his head and pleaded, "Yes, oh! Right there. Oh, Dax...."

He knew just what to do, to make the ecstasy last. He found the right spot and he played it. She would rise, eager, urgent, reaching for the finish.

And then he would ease off, go slower. The waterfall's edge of her building climax would retreat.

She begged him. She was shameless. She grabbed for his big shoulders, she curved her fingers into his thick, silky hair, digging her heels into the blankets, pushing her hungry body up to him, needing the fulfillment that his skilled mouth was promising, careful only of the bandage on his forehead. "Please. Oh, Dax. Please..."

But he wouldn't give in and give her what she begged for, not until stars danced behind her eyes and her body hummed and quivered and she felt the glow of her own arousal all through her, in each deep, hungry beat of her heart, across every inch of her heated, sweat-dewed flesh.

Finally, he let it happen. She spun toward the waterfall, her whole body alive, shimmering, supersensitized. She spun toward it—and miracle of miracles—she went over.

In a glorious free fall, she cried out his name as the pleasure rose up and consumed her, in a shimmer of falling jeweled brightness, of pure physical joy.

Of wondrous completion.

He slid up her body as she came. His mouth, wet with her excitement, hot from those endless kisses, pressed a burning, slick trail over her quivering belly, across the white fabric of her T-shirt, along the sweat-damp column of her exposed throat. He took her mouth with a groan.

And he entered her.

Just like that. She let out a sound of surprised fulfillment. She had no clue when he'd freed himself of his pants, of his boxer briefs.

But he *was* free. She reached down and took his hard, naked hips between her hands.

It was perfect, just what she needed, his mouth on hers in a never-ending kiss, the feel of him filling her, gliding in so hot and hard and slick as the last sweet pulses of her climax beat around him, easing his way.

"So good. Zoe…" He breathed her name into her mouth.

She took it, took all of him, all the way. And she sucked his tongue into her mouth as she lifted her hips to him, eager and ready for each hard, hungry thrust.

They rolled, moaning, kissing, and she was on top. It felt so good, so right. She reared up above him and rode him, rocking her hips on him, claiming each hot, perfect sensation as it rolled into her and through her, and onward, like a rushing, brilliant burst of light, out her toes, her fingertips, the top of her head.

And then, somehow, the bright light of her pleasure whirled in the close air around them and came back into her, expanding, sliding along each and every nerve ending.

Until another climax approached. She shuddered, crying out, and her body collapsed on top of him.

She came yet again, a swift, searing explosion of sensation, as he claimed the top position once more, braced up on his powerful arms and let his own climax have him.

He gazed down at her, his dark eyes so soft and low and gleaming, the bandage white as snow against his forehead, as he pulsed within her, and her body welcomed him, urging him deeper, harder, faster.

At the very end, he tossed his head back. A low, deep growl rose in his chest. His big arms gave way and he came down to her again, locking his mouth to hers, kissing her so deeply, still expanding and contracting within her.

And for the third time, her body answered, going over the waterfall yet again and then slowly, deliciously drifting down into the pool of contentment below.

Some time passed. She stroked his lean hips, eased her fingers under the shirt he still wore to learn the powerful, slick musculature of his beautiful back.

He kissed her cheeks, her chin, her throat, little wet,

nipping kisses, that made her shiver in the most lovely, delicious way.

But then, ripping through the lazy aftermath of pleasure like the slashing arc of a sharp, sharp knife, the realization hit her. She grabbed his shoulders, pushed him away, made him look at her.

He blinked those bedroom eyes. "What?"

"The condom. We didn't.…"

He chuckled.

She stared up at him, appalled. "You're laughing. We forgot the condom and you are laughing about it."

"Zoe…" He kissed he nose.

She punched him in the shoulder. "Don't you dare kiss my nose. Do you realize—?"

"Zoe, it's okay. I didn't forget."

She was midway into punching him again. That second punch, she pulled. "You didn't forget." She blew out a breath of pure relief. "Whew."

"See?" He lifted up enough that she could look between their bodies.

She saw, marveled, "How did you do that? I had no idea…"

He settled on top of her again and kissed the curve where her shoulder met her neck, whispered against her damp skin, "I'm not going to say years of practice. It wouldn't sound the least romantic."

She was able to laugh, too, then. She wrapped her arms around him and planted a big, loud smacker of a kiss on his beard-scratchy cheek. "Oh, I cannot tell you how relieved I am."

He rolled a little, so they were facing each other, but wrapped a muscular, hairy leg across her and somehow managed to stay inside. "That's one thing you don't have to worry about with me, one thing I never forget."

She stroked the side of his face. "Well, that's good. That's very good."

He tucked her closer, tighter in his arms. She shut her eyes and drifted, satisfied. Content for the first time in what seemed like a lifetime.

Some minutes later, he gently rolled away. "Don't go anywhere." He kissed her forehead, smoothed her hair.

Half-asleep, she yawned. "Not a problem. I'll be right here."

He left the tent. She sank back into slumber until he returned, zipping the tent flaps after him. She heard him rustling around next to her, pulling off the rest of his clothes.

And then he came back down to her and gathered her close, spoon-fashion. It was a wonderful sensation, to have him curved around the back of her, touching her everywhere.

She felt his lips against her neck and his hand gliding up under shirt.

He whispered, "This shirt, this bra…they're in my way."

She could feel him, unfurling, against her back. "You are insatiable."

"I try." He had the shirt by the hem and he was pulling it upward. She stretched out her arms and let him take it away. The bra went next and finally, they were both completely naked.

He guided her over onto her back. She opened her eyes lazily and, in the hazy glow from the banked fire outside, they regarded each other.

"Good," he said.

She nodded. "Very good."

And then he lowered his dark head to her breast.

They made love again, slowly, less urgently than the first time—but no less passionately.

After that, he pulled her into the circle of his arms and they slept.

In the morning before dawn, they added wood to the smoke pit, applied insect repellent and went to the river while the fish were biting. Dax caught two again in no time. She cleaned them and they returned to camp.

They ate breakfast. He shaved and changed the wrap on his forehead, which was healed enough now to take two big bandages rather than the more complicated dressing of gauze and tape.

They were discussing the various possible activities of the day—bathing in the river, making love endlessly, foraging for edible plant life to supplement their diet of fish and dried snake—when Dax put up a hand for silence.

"Shh. Hear that?"

She listened, shook her head—and then froze. Her mouth dropped open. Could it really be? At last? "Oh, Dax. I do hear it. It's a plane!"

Chapter Nine

The sound was coming closer from the south, the steady growl growing louder.

"A small plane," Dax said. "Single engine. The flares?" He wobbled upright on his good foot and threw more wood on the fire.

She jumped from her chair and sprinted the few steps to the plane. The flares waited on the floor of the front seat where she'd put them when Dax was so sick.

She grabbed two. By then, the plane was directly overhead. She tossed a flare to Dax, lit hers as he caught his and lit it, too.

They waved the flares, yelled as loud as they could.

The plane kept on going.

They stood there, looking up, still holding the sizzling flares, waiting for the sound of it to grow louder again as it circled back. Her heart was beating so hard and fast, it felt as if it might punch through the wall of her chest.

The drone of the small engine faded away toward the north. Still, they waited. Maybe it would take a few minutes for the pilot to turn around.

More waiting. Awful, agonizing waiting.

And nothing.

They looked at each other then and both said the same really bad word at the same time.

Her heart slowed, dragging now. It found the sad rhythm of disappointment. The adrenaline spike faded, making that sick, dropping feeling in the pit of her stomach.

She stuck her still-fizzing flare in the ground and Dax did the same with his. Then she asked, hopefully, "You think they saw us?"

He shrugged. "The odds are pretty good—the clearing is highly visible from the air. Not to mention the wrecked plane, the fire. The two of us, waving our arms like mad. Plus, the flares— Yeah, I'm thinking they saw us, definitely."

"So maybe they'll report our location to the authorities at least?"

"I have no idea. But it is a little odd they didn't circle back, just to make sure."

She nodded, muttered another bad word and said half to herself, "Drug smugglers, maybe…"

He was shaking his head. "You just never know."

She sank to her camp chair. "All these days…Monday to Sunday. Seven days—and nothing. And finally a plane goes over, and then right on by. I was kind of getting used to our situation, learning to live with it…."

He limped near and stood above her. "Come up

here." When she rose, he took her in his arms, kissed her hair, caught her face between his hands and kissed the tip of her nose.

She asked morosely, "Are you trying to cheer me up?"

"Is it working?"

"Well, a little…"

He held her gaze. "You're the one who's always reminding me that we can't afford to let our attitudes slip."

"You're right. You're absolutely right."

"And it's possible they didn't *need* to come back around, that they have our coordinates and help will be on its way. It's not as if anyone would try and land here unless they were in a helicopter or, like us, they had no other choice. So buck up."

"Yes, Dax."

"We're going to have ourselves a great time. Fishing, swimming, having all the sex we want together. Digging for grubs and root vegetables—"

"Dax."

"What?"

"Just leave it at the endless sex, okay? Quit while you're ahead."

Keeping the fire going a little higher than usual and the flares close at hand, they went about their day.

Zoe got out her cameras and carried them with her—to the river, along the other trails that led off the clearing. She didn't want to miss her chance to get some decent pictures, in case they did get out soon.

She took a lot of photographs that day, including any number of private photos of Dax, just for herself. And she took many more that would be suitable for general distribution—not only of him, but of the shy crocodile basking in the sun on the far riverbank, of a bright blue macaw perched on a palm leaf, of the waterfall in all its churning, jeweled glory.

But no more planes went over. The rescue helicopter they hoped for never appeared. And no one came out of the jungle to tell them they were saved.

As they ate their dinner of grilled fish, steamed bamboo shoots and baked yams, he said, "It's very possible that the people who live in this area actually know we're here."

She glanced around at the rim of dark trees and then called, "Hey, if you're out there, take us to your leader! Please!"

He chuckled. "If they haven't shown themselves so far, your shouting at them probably isn't going to do it."

"But why wouldn't they show themselves?"

"How would I know? Maybe they don't trust us, maybe others like us have made them wary—rich Anglo-Americans, who think they own the world. It's possible they'll decide to come forward eventually."

"And it's also possible there's simply no one there."

He shrugged, tipped his head up to the black, star-strewn sky. "Mostly, it seems that way, doesn't? Like we're the only two people left on Earth."

Not much later, they crawled into the tent together. In the fading light from the fire, she took a few more private pictures of him, pictures just for herself.

And then he told her to put her camera away.

She obeyed without argument. She went into his waiting arms.

And she was set free of the thousand and one fears

that haunted her constantly: that they wouldn't be rescued, that some deadly predator would finish them off first; that some death-dealing illness or injury would befall one or the other of them, leaving only one left.

Alone.

Somehow, that terrified her the most—that something might happen to him. She would lose her only companion. Secretly, since the crash, she had prayed that if one of them had to die, it would be her.

Partly because she found she had begun to care for him way too much. And partly because she was selfish; she didn't think she could bear being left all alone.

Yet in the tent that night, there was only his kiss, only the marvelous terrain of his fine body. Only his passion.

And hers.

After they made love, they talked. He was so easy to talk to. And here, away from SA and the constraints of his role as Dax Girard, über-rich ladies' man and macho adventurer, he was honest with her, revealing himself in ways he might never have done back at home.

He said that his workaholic father had died of a heart attack a month after Dax got his master's from Yale. The death of his distant yet adored dad changed everything, he said.

"All my life, I had waited, to be a grown-up, for him to respect me and pay attention to me. He died without that ever happening."

When his father died, Dax swore he would never be like the old man, ignoring the important things, never traveling, never really enjoying any of the pleasures of life, working himself into an early grave.

She stroked his shoulder, feeling sad for him. Without

a mother at five, losing his father in his early twenties. "So…who's Nora?"

He pressed a kiss against her hair. "When did I mention Nora?"

"You called out to her, more than once, when you were so sick."

"Nora was my wife," he said. "We married when we were both still in school."

"She's not…?" Zoe hesitated to say the word. He'd lost his mother and his dad so young. Surely his wife hadn't died, too.

"She's alive and well, happily remarried, with the children she always wanted."

That was a relief. It was too bad that their marriage hadn't lasted. But at least his wife hadn't died on him, too. "What happened—I mean, that you're not still together?"

"She wanted kids. I didn't. And then, when we were married barely a year—this was about four months before my father died—she got pregnant."

"Whoa. I had no idea you had a child."

"I don't."

"Well, then…?"

"The baby's heart didn't develop properly. She was born prematurely and they couldn't save her."

"Oh, Dax. I'm so sorry…"

Gruffly, he commanded, "Don't be sorry for me. Be sorry for Nora. It was terrible for her. She never forgave me."

"Wait a minute. It was *your* fault that your daughter died?"

"I didn't want children. I didn't want them ever, I realize now. Being a dad is just not what I'm looking for, not what I'm cut out for. Nora knew it. And we had agreed to wait a few years, until I thought I was ready. But then she got pregnant. I wasn't happy about it. And I told her so—after which I realized what a complete ass I was being, and apologized. I put a smiling face on it, told her it would all work out. And then I tried to accept that a baby was coming, that I had to settle down and learn to be the father I'd never wanted to be. She knew what was really going on inside me, knew that no matter how hard I tried to accept what was happening, I felt trapped."

"And so, when she lost the child…"

"She resented me. And I really can't say I blame her. No, I didn't cause the baby's death. But Nora knew damn well I wasn't looking forward to being a dad—plus, she couldn't understand the sudden change in me after my father died. She used to say I had a strange, far-away look in my eyes. As if I wanted to be anywhere but with her, with the baby she was having. And she was right. It wasn't anything she'd done. She was a beautiful, kind, loving woman. It just turned out we wanted completely different things out of life."

"And after the divorce…that was when you began to travel the world?"

He made a low sound, a thoughtful sort of noise deep in his throat. "At first, I traveled to console myself, to get past the guilt of failing at my marriage, of losing that baby I never really wanted, the little girl who died without drawing breath. I was trying to escape the reality of how completely I had disappointed Nora—and myself. But soon enough, I was traveling because I loved it so much.

"After the pain and loss faded, that was a great time for me. I would live in the finest luxury resorts one week and disappear into the wilds the next."

"So where does *Great Escapes* come in?"

"Eventually, I realized I did have a need for productive activity, for work that matters to me. Remember that ne'er-do-well uncle of mine?"

"I do."

"He'd taken me to San Antonio a couple of times during my Texas visits. And I'd loved it there. So I moved to SA, started the magazine. No, it doesn't make me any richer. My investments do that. But it's a job tailored exactly to my talents and my affinities. I travel the world and I write about it in *Great Escapes*."

Zoe was still certain that if—*when*—they got back home, they would, as agreed, go back to their strictly professional relationship. She needed *not* to get her hopes up that Dax might turn out to be the man for her in any long-term way.

Still, she couldn't stop herself from asking, "So… you ever think you might get married again—say, when you're ninety and too old for anything but rocking in your rocking chair and loving some lucky old lady?"

"Never again," he said softly. But he meant it.

"Children?"

"Without a wife?"

"Well, it does happen."

"Not to me. I'm no family man—married or otherwise. I know myself better now, know my limitations, know what I want from life. Marriage and/or a family… it's not going to happen."

She felt a small twinge and recognized it for what it was: regret. In spite of her determination not to, she *had* been nurturing some small spark of hope, for a possible future with him beyond this, and beyond *Great Escapes*. She could see now that it really wasn't to be.

The small spark flickered and died.

And she told herself she wasn't disappointed. She'd known going in that he wasn't marriage material. And besides, a husband was the last thing she was looking for at this point.

So it was all good. Wicked good.

The next day was Monday, their anniversary in the clearing. A whole week and they had survived to celebrate it.

Again, Zoe carried her cameras everywhere. She took at least as many pictures as she had the day before.

After dinner, as darkness claimed the sky, Dax produced a carefully packed bottle of Scotch from one of his suitcases. It was to have been a gift for Ramón Esquevar.

"I think," Dax said, "that under the circumstances, Ramón will understand if we open it without him." The label said it was aged fifty years.

It went down hot and smooth and smoky. "Delicious," Zoe said. "I can't believe I'm sitting here in the jungle with you, drinking Scotch that's almost as old as my mother."

He laughed and asked her about her family, about what it was like growing up a Bravo. She described each of her brothers, her sister, her half sister, the various spouses and children.

A slow smile curved his tempting mouth. "And now, I want the real dirt. I want to know what makes Zoe Bravo tick."

It didn't even occur to her to hold back—not here, not now. "I'm the family's 'free spirit,' the one who never figured out what she wanted to do in her life. I used to be perfectly happy about that, about getting by off the income from my trust fund, about not being tied down to earning a paycheck, not having that ingrained need to make a so-called 'success' of my life. I had no issues with simply moving on if something—like school or a job—started getting tiresome."

He picked up on the operative words. "Used to? Past tense?"

She treated herself to another slow sip of Ramón Esquevar's excellent Scotch. "Yeah, it finally got old. It got so when my dad called me his little free spirit, I wanted to punch his lights out. I knew then—like you, when you created *Great Escapes*—that I needed to find work I could stand doing on a daily basis."

"And now you have." He raised his tin cup.

She tapped hers against it. "To work."

"And to you, Zoe Bravo. I can't tell you how glad I am that you showed up in my office that fateful Thursday in June. There is no one I'd rather be stranded in the jungle with, no one in the whole damn world, and that is a fact."

"Back at ya, Dax, and then some."

They sipped, slowly, savoring every drop.

That night, in the tent, after lovemaking even more satisfying than the night before and the night before that, she laughed and warned that at this rate, they were going to run out of condoms before the rescue he so adamantly predicted could occur.

"I doubt it." He was downright smug. "I brought plenty."

"Always prepared."

Braced up on an elbow, he traced a circle around her navel. "I don't want any surprises. So I make it my business to prevent them."

"Then again…"

"Is that a criticism I hear coming?"

"Well, Dax, if you really want to protect yourself against those kids you say you're never going to have, why not get a vasectomy?"

Did she expect the question to give him pause?

It didn't. He bent close just long enough to press a soft kiss on the vulnerable flesh of her belly. Then he shrugged. "You're absolutely right. And I've been to the urologist more than once to get it done."

"But?"

He shook his head. "I always chicken out. Some ingrained macho idea I have of myself, I think. That I'll somehow be less a man if I'm sterile."

"You know that's just crap, right?"

He idly stroked her shoulder. "Yes, I do know. Still, it's crap that I haven't gotten past yet."

She couldn't resist suggesting, "Then maybe you do want to have kids, someday. Somewhere deep in your macho manly man heart, I mean."

"No, I don't." He sounded very sure. "I've just got a stupid, irrational fear of being less of a man. A fear I *will* get over, one of these days."

Zoe reached up to cradle the side of his dear face. "You know, I could actually start to admire you if things keep on like this."

He faked a look of dismay. "You don't already? What is *wrong* with you?"

She laughed, but then she grew serious again. "You're more honest and self-aware than I realized."

"High praise."

"Yeah, who knew? Sheesh. That first day, during the interview, I was actually thinking that working for you was the last thing I ought to be doing."

He ran a finger slowly down the outer edge of her

arm, bringing a little shiver in anticipation of future pleasures. "Yeah, I'm a lousy interviewer, I know. I need to work on that."

"No kidding." She did a bad imitation of Dax's deep voice. "'Can I be straight with you? You work for me, that's *all* you do with me....'"

He had the grace to look chagrined. "Yeah, that was a little over the top."

"A little?"

"See it from my point of view. I had just lost two assistants in a row, had to let them go when they decided they were in love with me. One of them showed up at my house unannounced, her arms full of gourmet food she'd whipped up just for me. She pushed past me into the house, set the bags of food on the entry table and then grabbed me in her arms and passionately declared that she had brought me dinner and we had to quit lying to ourselves. We had to face that we were meant for each other."

She tried not to laugh. "Oh, no."

"Oh, yes. And the next one was worse. I got off the elevator one morning and she wasn't at her desk. She was at mine. *On* mine, in fact, and wearing nothing but a sexy pout and pair of red high-heeled shoes."

"I can just picture it—and I really wish I couldn't."

"So I had to fire her, too. It was very inconvenient. She cried. She talked about filing a lawsuit, about getting a restraining order on me."

"On *you?* But *she* was the one who—"

He bent close for a quick kiss. "You're preaching to the choir, Zoe."

"What did you do?"

"I gave her a big severance package—and told myself

I was one lucky SOB that I could afford to pay her off. She finally went away."

Zoe teased, "An inconvenient naked woman. Is there anything worse?"

He traced a finger down the side of her throat, the caress feather-light. "Somehow, when you say 'naked' and 'woman' in the same sentence, it doesn't seem like that could ever be a bad thing."

She caught his hand, kissed it. "But it was."

"Yeah."

"You needed someone who could keep her mind on the job."

"Exactly. So when you came along, I decided to get it crystal clear in the interview that a hot affair would not be happening. And then right away I regretted making such a big deal about it. I realized I wouldn't have minded at all if I'd come in one morning and found *you* naked on my desk."

She held his gaze. "I'm flattered, you know that. But—"

"I know." He looked resigned as he pulled his hand from hers. "Never would have happened. Never *going* to happen, not when we get back to civilization. We have an agreement and I promise to stick by it."

"Well, all right, then."

He leaned closer. In the faint glow from the fire outside, his dark eyes were full of sensual promises. "So I guess I'd better grab my chance while I've got you naked in my arms, huh?"

"I guess you'd better." She reached up, combed the hair at his temple with her fingers. "Kiss me, Dax."

And he did kiss her—everywhere. When he rolled on the condom and eased himself between her open thighs, she thought that being lost in the jungle was almost worth the fear they might not make it out. She could live with the fear.

As long as she had Dax in her arms every night.

She woke to the strangest sound. Like the beating wings of a giant bird.

Her eyes flew open. Daylight. It was morning. Dax was already up, bent over beneath the low roof of the tent, hopping around on his good foot, getting into his pants.

"Wh—what's going on?" she muttered thickly, her mind still lost in a fog of sleep.

"Helicopter," he said the impossible word as he zipped up his pants. "It's happening, Zoe."

"Uh. Happening?"

"We're being rescued."

"Rescued..." Could it really be?

It was. The beating wings were descending—coming closer, louder. The sides of the tent rippled in a sudden hard wind.

Dax granted her his wonderful heartbreaker's smile. "Better put some clothes on, don't you think?"

Chapter Ten

Zoe got her clothes on in record time.

They went out and stood by the glowing coals of last night's fire as the helicopter touched down toward the north end of the clearing. A man jumped out of the passenger side while the giant, whipping blades still whirled, dangerously fast.

It was her dad.

Davis Bravo wore old jeans and battered boots and a T-shirt. And to Zoe, he looked like everything safe and comforting and strong in the world. The recent years of anger and frustration with him fell away. He was only her dad, the best dad in the whole wide world.

He ran at a half-crouch, ducking beneath the spinning blades until he cleared them. When he stood tall again, she was already launching herself at him.

She landed like a bullet against his broad chest. He

didn't so much as stagger. He wrapped his arms around her tight and hugged her so close.

And in a broken voice, against her hair, he murmured, "Zoe. My little girl. Thank God. Zoe..."

She was crying, the tears smearing on her cheeks, dripping down her chin. "It's okay, Dad. I'm okay. We're safe, we're well."

Slowly, he released her. His ice-green eyes were wet. He swiped an arm across them. "Your mother is going to be the happiest woman alive. She's been in bad shape—we all have...." He choked up.

She sniffed, loudly, dashed away her own tears. "Well, you found me at last. And I'm so very glad."

He clasped her shoulder, as if he needed the contact, the proof that only touch could give him that she really was standing right there in front of him. He cleared his throat and sought the words—and then shook his head.

She understood. He was too choked up to speak right then.

His gaze shifted to just behind her. She sensed that Dax was there and she sent him a joyous smile over her shoulder.

"Dax," her dad got out gruffly.

"I can't tell you how good it is to see you, Davis."

"Thank you," her dad said, "for keeping my little girl safe."

Dax took her father's offered hand. "Your little girl can take care of herself. She saved my life."

Her dad laughed then. "She's something special all right. And I'm so glad to see that you're both in one piece."

"We're all right, Davis. Even better, now you're here."

* * *

The helicopter had space for most of their luggage. They packed it in, knowing that anything they had to leave behind was probably lost for good.

When they climbed on board and the pilot lifted off, Zoe stared down at the clearing below.

She drank it all in: the battered shell of their brave little plane; the campfire she had built herself while Dax was so sick that she feared he would die; the yellow tent where they had made such beautiful love, held each other so close, told each other truths they never would have revealed under different circumstances.

She felt a wrenching tug on her heartstrings. A sadness so deep it almost doubled her over as it welled up beneath the pure joy of seeing her dad again, of knowing that they really had been rescued, as Dax had always insisted they would.

So much had happened down there. Awful things. Wonderful things. And she had lived to tell about it, lived to go home. Strange how now she was leaving, now she was free at last of the nagging fear that they wouldn't make it out, she missed it already.

Missed it all—the good *and* the bad.

She turned to the man sitting beside her, saw in those beautiful bedroom eyes that he knew. He got exactly what was going on here. They were gaining their lives again. And to do that, they had to leave something precious behind.

They had to turn their backs on the Zoe and Dax who had created their own private world apart, down there together, in the clearing. The real world was waiting for them.

Each of them knew who the other really was now. They understood each other.

They had their agreement in place and the time had come to keep it.

As it turned out, their Cessna's forced landing had happened farther south than they'd calculated. The plane had gone down about sixty land miles northeast of the Chiapan state capital of Tuxtla Gutiérrez, where they were supposed to have landed in the first place. The helicopter ride wasn't long.

Davis had radioed ahead. Zoe's mom and an ambulance were waiting for them when they got there.

Aleta cried unashamed tears of joy as she held out her arms to her youngest child. Zoe went into them gratefully, still in Mexico, yes—but in her heart, where it mattered most, already home.

There was a ride to the hospital. Zoe was quickly pronounced in good health. They X-rayed Dax's ankle, checked his head injury and came up with the expected prognosis. His ankle was sprained, healing well. The gash on his forehead would leave a jagged scar unless he opted for a few visits to a plastic surgeon.

Once the doctor said they were good to go, a couple of official-looking types appeared to interview them about their ordeal. Since they had all the necessary paperwork to show the two men, it was strictly a routine meeting. A plane had gone down in a bad storm and somehow both occupants had survived. There were *i*'s to dot and *t*'s to cross.

Next, they headed for a four-star hotel, where large, airy rooms waited for them. Zoe went straight to hers. She showered off the jungle grime and then sat in a scented bath for over an hour.

She was just getting dressed again when her mom showed up to take her to the hotel spa. Gratefully, Zoe let the pros go to work on her. By the time they were finished with the mineral body scrub, fresh color for her hair and the spa mani-pedi, she felt ready to face the world again.

Dax also disappeared for most of that day. Beyond cleaning up, he had a lot of calls to make, to *Great Escapes,* to Ramón Esquevar, to any number of others. He had business to catch up on and he had to contact the insurance people and also to see about getting a cleanup crew out to the ruined plane. Zoe *had* offered to help him with all of it, but he had ordered her to take some personal time and he wouldn't listen when she insisted she didn't mind giving him a hand.

That night, Davis, Aleta, Zoe and Dax shared a celebratory meal in the hotel's best restaurant. Zoe thought how handsome Dax looked, perfectly groomed in a white tropical-weight shirt and sand-colored trousers, carrying a new cane—ebony, with a silver handle. She tried not to stare at him longingly and thought she managed pretty well.

When it was time to turn in, Zoe went to her room and Dax retired to his.

Zoe stripped down and soaked in the big tub again—because it was there, because she could. The bed was soft as a cloud, the sheets about a gazillion thread count. She felt light-years away from the tent in the jungle.

And achingly lonely for Dax's body pressed close to hers.

She knew his room number, but she didn't go to him. She didn't pick up the phone to call him—or if she did, she set it quietly back in its cradle without dialing.

This was the toughest part: tonight, the next night.

Maybe for a week or two. Gradually, it would get easier. She wouldn't yearn for his arms around her, for the touch of his lips on hers, for the feel of his breath as it stirred her hair.

She wouldn't miss him so desperately. These needful feelings would pass. She would be fine.

If she had learned nothing else from the jungle ordeal, she had learned that she knew how to endure.

The next day, Wednesday, her dad had one of the BravoCorp jets take them back to San Antonio.

There were reporters waiting on the tarmac when they landed. The media wanted the scoop on Dax Girard's latest big adventure, on the thrilling rescue of a daughter of one of San Antonio's first families. For ten minutes or so, they answered shouted questions, about what it had been like, how they had lived through it and what they had felt when help came at last.

When the reporters finally let them pass, Dax left her without a soft word or a single touch—which was fine, she told herself. Just what she wanted. They were back to life as they had known it before the crash.

"Take the rest of the week off," he commanded. "Catch up on whatever you need to catch up on. I'll expect you back in the office bright and early Monday morning."

As if. "Thanks. I would like a day. So I'll take tomorrow for myself, if that's all right with you."

He didn't miss a beat. "Good, then. See you Friday." He turned to shake her father's hand and to kiss her mother's cheek. "Davis, thank you for everything. And Aleta, what can I say?"

Her mom beamed up at him. "You can say that you'll come to dinner at our family's ranch, Bravo

Ridge. Sunday afternoon about three? Let my family show their appreciation for what good care you took of Zoe."

He smiled his killer smile. "I think it was the other way around, to be honest. *She* took care of *me*."

Her mom was not letting him charm his way out of her invitation. "Please. Sunday? Zoe will give you directions."

Zoe tried to help him say no. "Mom, come on. He's a busy man and—"

He didn't let her finish. "You know, I think I would enjoy that. Absolutely, I'll be there." Did he slant Zoe a challenging glance?

She had no idea because she refused to look at him. "Well, okay, then," she chirped out, falsely bright. "Great."

"See you Friday," he said again, speaking directly to Zoe that time.

She made herself meet his eyes. It wasn't easy. "Thank you, Dax. For everything."

"Nothing to thank me for." His voice was brusque. "We both know that. Without you, I'd be dead."

She thought of that giant snake dropping out of the trees above her head and suppressed a shudder. "Back at ya." They were the words they had said to each other in the jungle. And they came out in a near-whisper.

He nodded and ducked into the limo that waited for him.

"What an amazing man," said her mother as the big, black car rolled off. She turned to Zoe with her most loving, coaxing smile. "Come on to the ranch with us, just for an hour or two? The family will have gathered to welcome you home."

She couldn't refuse an invitation like that, even if

she'd wanted to—which she didn't. "Of course. I would love it. I can't wait to see everyone."

So they drove out to Bravo Ridge.

The whole family was there. When their driver pulled to a stop in front of the wide-spaced white pillars that lined the long verandah, the front door opened and everyone came pouring out.

It was 2:00 p.m. on a weekday, but each of her hard-charging brothers had taken the afternoon off to see her safe at home again—even Travis, who hardly ever came in from his latest oil derrick. He'd driven up from the Gulf just to give his baby sister a hug.

Zoe was handed from one set of loving arms to the next.

Her niece, Kira, even demanded a big hug of her own. She held up her sweet little arms. "Aunt Zoe, Aunt Zoe, me, too! I missed you. I was so worried because you were lost. Hug me, too!"

So Zoe scooped her up and spun her around and drank in the feel of those small arms clasped tight around her neck.

When she let Kira down, she smoothed a hand over her short golden hair, reluctant to relinquish the moment. And she thought of what it might be like, to have a little girl of her own.

Strange. To picture herself as a mother—and not just in a hypothetical sense, but in a true awareness that she wanted that, wanted a baby of her own someday.

Dax had done that, made her see herself and her dreams of her future all the more clearly—at the same time as she realized that her dreams weren't *his* dreams. When she did have children, they wouldn't be Dax's. He didn't want to get married, ever. He didn't want children. He'd been totally honest and up-front about that.

She needed, above all, to keep in mind that a relationship between them could go nowhere, even if she were willing to put the job she loved in jeopardy for the chance to be with him again.

Zoe stayed at the ranch, with her family around her, through an early dinner and most of the evening. Her dad and mom dropped her off at her condo on their way home.

Everything at her place was just as she'd left it. Even her houseplants had done fine in her absence. She'd put them in trays of water before she left and they'd come through looking as perky as they had on the day of her departure.

It was almost ten. But she didn't feel sleepy. And Dax had given her the next day off. She put her cameras, her laptop and her PDA on their chargers and unpacked. Just about everything was dirty. So she sorted laundry and started the first load.

Then she got the memory cards from her cameras and uploaded the pictures she'd taken onto her home PC. Some of them were really good.

And a large number of them were of Dax—at the river, basking on a rock, looking like everything a man should be. And by their campfire, putting their fish dinner on the grill, giving her a big thumbs up. She had pictures of him shaving in the morning, his face slathered in a white foam of shaving cream. Pictures of him checking the smoke pit, pictures of his fine, broad back as he hobbled ahead of her on the trail to the river, leaning on his makeshift cane.

There were pictures of him in the tent, too. Naked. Eyes low and lazy. She looked at those for a long time.

Mine, she thought. No one but she would ever see those pictures.

They were for her hungry eyes alone.

Once she'd uploaded all the photos to their own album in a private space online, she checked email. It was a good thing she still wasn't sleepy, because there were hundreds of new messages. She scanned them all quickly, checking for spam to dump first. The sixth-to-last message, sent at six-ten that night, was from Dax.

Thinking about you. Can't help it. Shoot me.

Her heart suddenly lighter, she typed, fast, *Thinking of you, too. Went out to the ranch to see my family. They're all looking forward to meeting you Sunday.*

She hesitated, her fingers poised on the keyboard. And then, before she could write something intimate, before she could step over the line they had drawn so carefully and clearly together, she hit the Send button.

And started again at the top of her inbox, deleting anything that didn't require a reply.

The little pinging sound happened a moment later: another email from Dax.

Her heart did the happy dance. It warmed her, touched her so deeply, to picture him sitting there at his computer, waiting for a message from her. It was almost as good as having his arms wrapped tight around her.

He'd written, *This is going to get better, right? Easier. Say it is, even if you're lying.*

She wrote back, *It is. I promise.*

His reply pinged back in less than sixty seconds. *Liar. Good night.*

Good night, Dax. She hit Send, her heart aching.

It took her an hour longer to finish dealing with

email. The whole time she sat at the PC, she was waiting, feeling edgy and out of sorts, hoping for another email from him, knowing that to wish for such a thing was totally unacceptable of her.

Over and over she reminded herself that these feelings would pass. She just needed *not* to give in to them. The task was to get through them, to ride them out.

Two new emails came in during that time. Neither was from him. She applauded his restraint.

She also wanted to beat her head against her keyboard in frustrated longing.

It was after two when she finally turned in. By then, all her laundry was washed and folded, her electronic devices freshly charged, her spam deleted, her inbox tidy, her text and phone messages handled.

Her life was in order. She'd gone down in the jungle and lived to tell about it; she was home and safe. Friday morning, she would return to the job she loved.

Too bad she felt so depressed. Too bad that no matter how many times she told herself she would get over Dax soon, she still had a big, fat hole in her heart, an empty, desolate space that felt as though it might never be filled.

She missed the clearing, missed the river and the waterfall and the shy crocodile. Missed the taste of smoked snake, of all things. Missed the yellow tent.

And more than any one of those things, more than the stunningly precious sum of that life-or-death experience, she missed the man who had shared it all with her.

Chapter Eleven

Lin was sitting on the edge of Zoe's desk, waiting for her, when Zoe got to the office first thing Friday morning. She held out her arms. "Get over here."

Zoe set Dax's coffee down and they shared a quick embrace.

"You lost weight." Lin stepped back and looked her up and down.

"Freeze-dried soup, bamboo shoots and snake meat. Very slimming."

"Still, you look pretty damn good, all things considered." Lin's sharp eyes spotted Zoe's ring finger. She grabbed Zoe's hand. "Omigod. What happened? You and Johnny...?"

"Long story. Lunch?"

"You're on."

The rest of the staff was already gathering around to welcome her back. They were quick about it and had left her to power up her computer and start getting her workday under way when the elevator doors slid open and Dax emerged.

Zoe ordered her silly heart to stop bouncing off the walls of her chest and handed him his coffee. "Good morning."

He leaned his cane against her desk and took off the lid, the way he always did. After sniffing it suspiciously, he condescended to a sip. "Good," he said.

She had no idea whether he meant the coffee or the morning. She supposed it didn't matter. He was there, three feet away from her, even if she couldn't throw her arms around him and take his mouth in an endless kiss.

She asked, "You got my directions to Bravo Ridge?"

He sipped again. "I saw you sent them. But I won't need them. We'll go together."

Joy leaped within her. She wished it would stop.

We'll go together. Was that wise? Probably not. But it certainly made sense. No need to take two cars, or to make him find the way on his own. Yes, it was dangerous, the two of them in a car, side-by-side, driving to her family ranch, the way any two people on an actual date might do.

But she was his assistant after all. They were going to be together a lot anyway. She needed to start getting used to being around him without being *with* him.

"I'll pick you up, then," she said.

"No, I'll drive."

She wanted to argue with him, say that she knew the way and he might as well ride with her. But she would only be picking a silly fight over nothing, seeking conflict with him as an outlet for her frustrated desire. "However you want it."

"That's what I like to hear."

"Say, two-fifteen?"

"That'll work." He grabbed his cane and disappeared into his office.

Thirty seconds later, he buzzed her. She got up and went in.

He looked up from typing something on his computer and his dark gaze ran over her, head to toe and back up again.

She felt weak in the knees, wet down below. It was absurd and she knew it. She had made her choice and she needed to stop indulging herself, stop wallowing in her own unsatisfied lust.

He said, "I'll need the pictures you took in the jungle. We're moving up a contributing editor's Spotlight to fill the slot for the January issue. I've decided to write the story of what happened in Chiapas as a special feature—don't worry, just the survival story. Not *our* story."

She didn't even try to hide her triumphant smile. "And you're using *my* pictures."

"Yeah, well. Are they any good?"

"Some of them are excellent. And I do realize it's a great opportunity...."

"But you want to be paid. And you should be. You will be." He named a very generous price. "That is, if they're usable."

"They are. And the price is right, thank you."

"Get with Jeffrey." Jeffrey Walleghar was the art director and the photo editor. "He'll give you the contract and see that you get the check."

"I'll do that."

He looked her up and down again. He wore the strangest expression. It wasn't a happy look. "You think you'll be the next Ramón Esquevar now?" Was he angry, for some reason?

Or simply frustrated and yearning for something he couldn't have? Just as she was.

She sat in the black club chair. "Dax, look. I know it doesn't work like that. It takes years to get to Esquevar's level. Most never get near that. And I'm good, but I'll never be that good. I enjoy photography, but in terms of a job, I like the editorial side better."

He leaned back, tossed his pen to the desk pad. "Are you reassuring me that I'm not going to lose you, is that it?"

"Yes. And I'm telling you that I don't want to be a full-time professional photographer. I want to be an editor. Maybe someday, an editor-in-chief."

"Don't get ahead of yourself."

She laughed. She couldn't help it. "I wouldn't dream of getting ahead of myself."

"Sure you would. Don't."

She wanted to ask him please not to be an ass, but that probably wouldn't be appropriate. "I'll have the pictures for you right away."

"Ten minutes? And we can do the huddle then."

"I'll be ready."

"Of course you will."

She left him, put the pictures on a memory stick and brought them back to him along with her laptop, ready for the huddle. He took the stick and they had their huddle, which went pretty smoothly, all things considered. There was a lot to catch up on, but he'd made a good start on it the day before.

After the huddle, she spent the morning getting on top of his correspondence, fielding the constant calls, dealing with catering for the two big meetings they were having that afternoon. The hours zipped by.

Before she knew it, Lin was standing over her, waiting to go to lunch.

They went to the coffee shop down the street. They ordered and waited for the food to come. Once the waitress had served them and left them alone, Lin got down to it.

"Okay, what happened with Johnny?"

Zoe told the truth. "There never was a Johnny. I bought a big, fake ring to get everyone off my back about falling for Dax."

Lin threw back her blue-streaked head and laughed out loud. "Oh, you are so bad."

"Well, it worked, didn't it?"

"It absolutely did. So…you busted yourself to Dax while you were lost in the jungle?"

"Yeah. Under the circumstances, the whole pretense started seeming beyond silly, not to mention no longer necessary."

"You and Dax had a thing, huh?"

Zoe kept a straight face. "What happens in the rainforest stays in the rainforest."

"That's not an answer."

"It's the only one I'm giving you."

Lin stuck her fork in her taco salad. "You are no fun at all, you know that? But still, I like you a lot and I'm glad you're here, safe."

"Me, too."

"Plus, Dax is getting so he can't function without you, so I guess it's just as well that you didn't fall hopelessly in love with him."

Hopelessly in love with him. Was she?

Lin was shaking her head. "Uh-oh."

She scowled. "What do you mean, uh-oh?"

"You should see your face."

"Eat your taco salad."

"You know what? You're right. It's time to change the subject. Your pictures are terrific. The feature is going to be a killer."

"I'm excited about it."

Lin forked up a big bite of salad, stuck it in her mouth, chewed and swallowed. "I'd still rather talk about you and Dax."

"It's not going to happen."

"I was afraid you'd say that."

When Zoe got back to her desk, Dax was in the first of his two afternoon meetings.

She went to work. There was no end of stuff to catch up on after almost two weeks away.

Dax reappeared at a little after three. "The pictures look good."

She stopped typing and grinned up at him. "Told you so. I know you sent them to Lin. She said at lunch that she likes them, too."

"I'm going to go on home now, see if I can finish the feature over the weekend." Below the giant bandage on his forehead, his eyes were dark and deep as ever, his nose as handsomely hawkish, his mouth an invitation to sin. If they were still in the clearing, she would rise and wrap her arms around him and tell him that he was the sexiest man alive. "Zoe?" Suddenly, his voice was husky, temptingly rough. "Did you hear what I said?"

She blinked. "Uh, yeah. Every word. You're going to finish the feature over the weekend."

"Is there…something you'd like to speak with me about privately?" His gaze spoke of agreements—of the hundred and one delicious ways they might be broken.

"Oh. No. Not a thing." She waved a hand, a gesture that failed to be as airy and unconcerned as she intended, mostly because she hit herself in the nose when she did it.

He grinned then.

Lin's fateful words echoed. *Hopelessly in love with him*.

Pull yourself together, a voice of steel within insisted. *Do it now.*

She sat up straighter, pushed the keyboard a little out of the way and folded her arms on the desk pad. "You were saying?"

There was a moment. They gazed at each other and so much was said without a word being uttered.

When he actually spoke, he was all business once again. "Play dragon lady as much as possible. Only forward my calls if something's on fire. And tell them all I'll be checking email periodically. Try to get them to reach me that way."

"Will do."

"See you Sunday."

"'Bye, then." She focused on her monitor again, put her hands on the keyboard and started her fingers moving. Still, she heard him walk away from her, was acutely aware of the sound the elevator doors made— sliding open and then shut.

When she knew he was safely gone, she let her flying fingers slow. She forgot all about the letter she was composing. Her gaze wandered forlornly to the shut elevator doors.

Hopelessly in love with him...

The phone on her desk rang. She answered it, took a

message, finished the letter she was typing. Proceeded to the next item on her endless to-be-done list.

Hopelessly in love with him.

She wanted to press her hands to her ears, shake her head, close her eyes tight and shout good and loud, over and over, *No, no, no, no!*

Anything to keep the scary words out.

Not that putting her hands over her ears would have done any good.

After all, the words were already inside her head.

She went out with girlfriends that night to celebrate her safe return. They went to Armadillo Rose, the bar her sister-in-law, Corrine—Matt's wife, Kira's mom—owned. The bar had belonged to Corrine's mother before her.

Matt had met Corrine there, at the Rose, fallen hard at first sight, or so the story went. Matt was a sweetheart. And also extremely pigheaded—a lot like Zoe's dad and more than one of her other brothers. It had taken him more than a few years to admit he was a goner, that Corrine was the only woman for him.

Weekends, the Rose always had a good band playing. It was a down-home kind of place. The bartenders were all female and easy on the eyes. They were also famous for getting up and dancing on the bar.

Corrine was there. Zoe caught her eye and waved her over. Corrine greeted her and her friends. "It's so good to have you home. First round's on the house."

"How about a pitcher of margaritas?"

"You got it."

When the pitcher came, Lisa Eppersill, Zoe's friend since middle school, offered a toast. "Here's to you, Zoe.

May the road, however twisty, always carry you back home."

Zoe thought of that last night in the clearing, when Dax broke out the bottle of very old Scotch and they toasted a full week of survival.

So what was *he* doing tonight, she couldn't help but wonder?

Slaving away at the feature story maybe?

Or enjoying an intimate evening with any one of a number of beautiful women who traveled in his glittering circle of friends and acquaintances?

It hurt, and bad. Like a knife, twisting hard and deep. To think of him with someone else.

And it didn't matter how sternly she reminded herself that she had known his reputation with women, had already seen him in action, when she decided to tinker with their strictly professional relationship in the first place. *She* had set the terms for their time in the clearing when they were lovers and for their return to civilization.

She had zero right to be hurt if he exercised his option as a single guy with no commitments. He was free to do the wild thing with a different gorgeous, sophisticated woman every night.

Even if the thought of his kissing someone else made her sick to her stomach—and furious, too.

"Dance?" A cute cowboy stood by their booth.

Zoe sent him a blinding smile as she realized he was talking to her. "Sure." She set down her margarita and got up to follow him out onto the floor.

When the dance was over, she rejoined her friends. The cowboy was not only cute but really sweet. It just wouldn't be right to use him to distract herself from the real issue.

Which was Dax and the growing likelihood that she actually had managed to fall hopelessly in love with him.

She got back to her condo at a little after midnight.

The first thing she did when she walked in the door was to dig around in her bag for her PDA, though she knew she shouldn't. Any texts or emails could certainly wait until morning. She ought to just leave it alone, refuse to check—as she'd been resolutely doing all evening.

There wouldn't be any email from Dax and there *shouldn't* be. And even if there was, she had no business checking her cell in the middle of the night just to see if there might be. She had to stop torturing herself. She had to let Dax go, move on. Or maybe, more correctly, go back.

To what they had been. Before the clearing.

Why wasn't that working for her? Why couldn't she just make an agreement and stick to it, for pity's sake?

Because you're hopelessly in love with him, that's why.

There *was* an email—two, as a matter of fact.

At 9:06: *I was going to pretend I needed to get with you about the feature story. But that would be a lie. I do need to get with you, Zoe. And it's not about the feature.*

And at 10:08: *You're out with some other guy, right? And I'm making a fool of myself. Okay, enough. Please disregard previous email.*

She didn't want to feel overjoyed and triumphant. But she did. On both counts. Her heart was suddenly light as a moonbeam in her chest.

Her thumbs flew over the BlackBerry's keys. *I just got in. I was out with some girlfriends. I don't want to disregard your email of 9:06. What I want is you, Dax. Here. In my arms.*

She hit Send before she could stop herself, before she let herself start remembering all the very valid reasons why she shouldn't.

Fifty-three seconds later, her cell rang. Now her bright moonbeam of a heart was lodged firmly in her throat.

Her hand shook as she punched the talk button.

Before she could even get out a hello, he asked, "Now?"

She had to cough to make her windpipe open up. "Um. I don't know if we…"

"Just answer the damn question, Zoe."

"I…"

"Say it."

What else was there to do in the end, but follow the dictates of her desire, of her foolish, yearning heart?

"Zoe, you're driving me crazy here. Just make up your mind."

"Sorry. Yes, Dax. Now."

Chapter Twelve

When she let him in the door, he braced his cane against the wall and reached for her.

She went into his arms, but then got a hand up between them and put it over his mouth so he couldn't kiss her. "We have to talk first."

He looked at her over the mask of her own hand, his eyes darker than ever, stormy as the afternoon their plane went down.

Sheepishly, she added, "Okay?" as she lowered her hand.

He made a noise in his throat. It was not a happy sound. "As if you even need to ask. As if *I'm* the one running this show." His arms felt like heaven around her. So good. So right.

Her body, accustomed to the feel of him, had been starved for his touch. It was everything, just to be held by him, just to breathe in the wonderful, sexy, delicious scent of him, to have him watching her with frank desire—and considerable annoyance.

"I have to say this, Dax."

"Get on with it, then."

"I thought I could do it, go back to the way it was before. I honestly did."

He tenderly caught a red curl that had fallen against her cheek and smoothed it back. "I know."

"But…well, for me, this thing between us is just too strong. I know you never want to get married or have kids, both of which I realize now I definitely do. I know that when it ends I will probably suffer on a number of levels. I'll be without you and I'll be out of a job I love. I know this is a bad idea. But I…I want you anyway. I want you really bad."

"Good." He put his hand under her chin, rubbed her lower lip with his thumb. It felt wonderful. Exciting. "And can you stop predicting what's going to happen later? Can we just go with what's happening now?"

He had a point, she thought. Who knew what might happen? She looked up into his beloved face and longed to ask him if he might, possibly, someday, be able to rethink his stance on marriage and kids.

But she didn't ask him any such thing.

If he was rethinking the whole family thing, he would tell her.

And she certainly didn't want to box him into a corner over it, the way his ex-wife had. She didn't want him to lie. He was…who he was. And she seriously needed to be mindful of that.

She *would* be mindful. But she wouldn't give him up. Not now.

Not yet.

She said, "And I think we should agree to keep it professional at work."

"Yes. I think so, too—are you going to let me kiss you now?" He dipped his head, tried to capture her mouth.

She turned away so it didn't happen. "And while it lasts, I want it to be exclusive. Just you and me. No other women."

He released her, took a step back. "I think I'm insulted."

"Dax." She closed the distance he'd put between them, laid her hands against his broad chest, felt the warmth of him—and the strength. "It needed to be said. I know women are constantly making plays for you. Beautiful, sexy, fascinating women. I want to know for certain that you can resist them. I want to know that, while you're with me, you're *only* with me."

"It's not an issue. Not after what happened, after what we've been to each other. I would be dead but for you. And if I hadn't been on that trail with you when you needed me, that big boa might have had you for dinner. I don't want some *stranger*, Zoe. I've been there and done that and believe me, I can resist. I want only you."

"Well." The word came out on a trembling sigh. "I guess that about says it all, doesn't it?"

"I damn well hope so." He lowered his head again.

That time she didn't turn away.

He took her mouth. She gave it up willingly, letting her hands slide up the hard contours of his chest to clasp around his neck, pressing her yearning body against him, tasting him, *knowing* him. Again.

Inevitable—it truly was. She saw that now. How futile and foolish of her to try to deny this.

There was no denying this. No judging the wisdom of it, no weighing the cost.

It simply was. Elemental. The way it had been in the clearing between them. The way it *had* to be, between them. Frank and real.

And burning hot.

His tongue speared into her mouth, grazing her teeth. She sucked on it hungrily. And when he retreated, she followed him. She relearned the slick flesh beyond his lips, shivered in arousal at the feel of his teeth, biting down just enough to excite her all the more.

It was so good, so exactly what she needed, what she'd been longing for.... And then he was scooping her up high against his chest.

"Your ankle!" she warned.

"It's fine," he growled.

She pointed the way to her bedroom and he took her there.

He set her down on the thick rug by her bed. And he undressed her, swiftly, peeling off the layers, tossing them aside, dipping to a knee to get her out of her Jimmy Choos, sweeping instantly to his feet again, hardly favoring his injured ankle at all now. He took down her short skirt and her panties. He pulled up the silk tank top she'd worn for her night out with the girls. She raised her arms and he took it away.

Her pink satin bra was the last to go.

"At last," he whispered, bending his head to her breast, sucking the nipple in, working it with his lips and his clever tongue, pinching it between his teeth so that she groaned and clutched him closer.

It felt so fine, as deeply satisfying as it was arousing, to hold him close to her, to gaze down through low-lidded eyes at his dark head against her breast in the pool of light from the bedside lamp. He was so good at lovemaking, he made her wild.

He guided her back onto the bed, joining her there, kicking his shoes off—she heard them thud onto the rug, one and then the other—as he went on kissing her breast.

She wanted him naked. Wanted to feel him, the whole strong, hot, muscled length of him in her arms, against her nude body. So she tugged at his shirt. He tried to ease her hands away.

She refused to let him do that.

"Off," she moaned, gripping handfuls of his shirt in tight fists. "I want your clothes off you. Now."

He let go of her breast and he looked up at her through those eyes that seemed to know every last one of her feminine secrets. His mouth was red, wet. He smiled. "You are the bossiest woman."

"Yes, I am." She gave a hard yank on the bottom of his knit shirt. "Now get out of this."

And he did. Just like that, he quit teasing her, quit putting her off. He raised his arms so she could pull the shirt off him, so she could reveal every delicious inch of his broad, tanned chest, his washboard belly. She gained the top position and she pushed him down onto the pillows. She unzipped his fly, pulled off his socks, took his trousers and his boxer briefs down.

He was so hard, curving up thick and strong out of the nest of dark hair. She wanted to touch him, to do everything to him, to imprint herself on his senses.

Until there was nobody else for him, until no other woman would ever do. So that later, when it was over, he would always remember, how right they had been together, how perfectly suited.

How very, very good.

"Satisfied?" One dark brow quirked.

"I plan to be."

He almost smiled. "I kind of figured that."

She touched him, traced the thick bulge of a vein that made a winding path along the length of him. And she watched his face as she did that. He wasn't smiling now. His eyes were softer suddenly, and his mouth, too. His breath came faster.

He said her name on a whisper, "Zoe…"

She wrapped her fingers around him, slowly, taking her time about it. She felt his groan as he tried to swallow it back. And then she stroked him, encircling him firmly, possessively—long and slow. Then faster. Then slow again. Varying the rhythm, purposely drawing out the sensual torture, watching his face as she played with him.

His eyes drooped closed. He gave himself up to her, to her touch, to her command.

She lowered her mouth to him, licked him, one long, tasting stroke.

He lifted his hips, groaned her name for a second time, whispered, "Yes. That. Yes.…"

So she took him inside, in a slow glide, going down to the base of him, relaxing her throat so she could get him all the way in.

By then, he didn't even try to stifle his moans of pleasure. He clutched the sheets, lifted his hips to her, eager for her, for the heat and wet of her mouth all around him. For the way she moved on him, up to the tip and down all the way—and then back up again, using her tongue and even her teeth just a little.

Until she knew he was close, right on the brink of his climax.

He went very still then. And he growled her name,

urgently, "Zoe. Wait." He touched her hair. "Be with me…please…"

Eager to feel him within her, she listened. One last wet stroke of her mouth and she let him go.

But then she remembered. "Condom. We forgot the—"

He lifted his right hand off the bed and turned it over. There it was, waiting in his palm.

She should have known.

He grinned. She grinned back.

And then he had it out of the wrapper and rolled down over him before she could stop him and tell him that she wanted to do it this time.

"Come here," he said rough and low. "Now."

She didn't argue. Not right then. They wanted the very same thing after all. She rose up to her knees and hitched her leg over him, straddling him.

He touched her then, and she allowed that. His knowing fingers stroked along the inside of her thigh, dipped between the neatly trimmed patch of chestnut hair, parting her.

Finding her already wet. Definitely ready.

Still, he eased a finger in, and then two. She rocked her hips, meeting and retreating from the skilled slide of his caress.

"Now?" he whispered.

"Oh, yes, Dax. Now…"

And he clasped her hips between his lean hands. She felt her own heated wetness on his fingers, cooling against her flank. She reached down to position him.

And then, with slow, deliberate intent, she lowered her body onto him, taking him into her, deep. And then deeper still.

She was primed for him, ready. She loved the way he felt within her, how perfectly he filled her.

He was watching her, his midnight gaze on her face. She met those eyes of his. She didn't look away.

Until the pleasure crossed the barrier into that place too close to ecstasy. Then, she let her head fall back. She let him slide his hands into the curve of her waist and upward, to cup her breasts, to tease them as she rode him.

And she let him pull her down onto him, breasts to chest. She accepted his kiss, a soul-deep kiss, and made no objection when he rolled her under him at the finish, claiming the dominant position.

She lifted her feet and hooked them around his rocking hips. She let him lead the way, over the edge.

Into the sparkling, endless free fall. Her body pulsed around him and he surged deep in answer.

As he spilled his climax into her, she lost herself in the spangled darkness of her own shattering fulfillment.

He stayed at her place that night. They slept as they had slept in the yellow tent, his body wrapped around hers, cradling her.

In the morning, she made them breakfast. She showered and dressed for the day. And he drove them to his place just outside SA, in an exclusive gated community.

His house was a mansion, sixteen thousand square feet, with a media room, private spa and exercise room, a master suite bigger than her whole condo—and just about every amenity known to man. His garage was the size of an airplane hangar, large enough to house his collection of classic and one-of-a-kind vehicles.

He had a gorgeous pool. The grounds were beautifully landscaped. There were ponds and charming winding paths, a roomy guest house, a tennis court.

When they went back into the main house, she teased him that he was the ultimate in conspicuous consuming.

He said, "You continue to fail to be impressed enough with all I have—not to mention all I am."

"Just remind me how you give a lot away to people who need it."

"You know that I do."

"Yes," she said softly. "I do know."

He *was* a generous man. He wrote whopping checks to more than one of the foundations her mother supported. Like the Texas State Endowment Fund, which provided needed goods and services for struggling families all over the state.

He took her hand. "Come up to my office. I want you to have a look at the Chiapas feature before I give it to Lin so she can chop it to pieces."

She read the feature while he had his shower. Reading his description of their forced landing, she felt like she was living through it all over again. And he'd done a truly stellar job of putting the reader in the story—without ever revealing their very personal relationship.

He came up behind her and put his hands on her shoulders just as she was finishing up the final paragraph. She felt his lips in her hair, smelled the moist, fresh-shaved scent of him.

"Well?" he demanded.

She sighed. "I would tell you all the things that are wrong with it…."

"I'm sure you will."

"I wish I could. Just to keep you humble."

He chuckled. "Me, humble? Like that's gonna happen."

"My thoughts, exactly." She spun the chair around, braced herself on the arms and pushed herself out of it enough to capture his mouth.

He did the rest, wrapping those heavenly arms of his around her, pulling her up and into his embrace.

They kissed. That took a while.

When he finally raised his head, she told him, "It's perfect. I wouldn't change a word."

They spent the rest of the day and that Saturday night together. And Sunday morning as well, returning briefly to her place so she could shower and change for the day.

In the afternoon, at the ranch, nobody seemed the least surprised that they arrived together. It turned out that everyone had already met Dax at one social or charity event or another, so it was more a matter of them all greeting him, thanking him for helping Zoe to get home safe, than of his being introduced.

He fit right in with the family. Zoe had pretty much expected he would. He was smart and funny and he was interested in other people, in how they saw the world, in what they thought and how they felt. That was part of what made him such a fine writer.

With Caleb, the family's top salesman, Dax talked cars. Caleb loved nothing so much as a fast, gorgeous automobile—well, except for his wife, Irina, who was tall and graceful and quietly regal. Caleb loved Irina more than anything, even a fast car.

With Luke, who ran the family ranch, Dax talked horses. With Gabe's wife, Mary, he talked writing. Mary wrote freelance for a number of different magazines, mostly articles on home life and ranching.

Abilene and Dax discussed architecture. He knew Donovan McRae, the world-famous architect who had offered Abilene that fellowship and then dropped completely out of sight, leaving Abilene frustrated, waiting for the "great man" to follow through.

Dax promised he would pull a few strings for her, try to find out what was up with Donovan.

"I read he was in some kind of ice climbing accident," Abilene said. "But then I heard he was all right. And whatever the problem is, well, I would be more understanding if I knew what was going on with him."

"I hear you," Dax agreed. "And this isn't like Donovan, to just drop off the radar like this—not with commitments hanging. I'll find out what I can and let you know."

He even listened with interest when six-year-old Kira cornered him and told him all about Rosie, the new puppy.

Zoe's mom said how pleased she was that he'd been able to come out to the ranch for the day. Aleta fairly glowed. At the dinner table, when Dax put his arm on the back of Zoe's chair and leaned close, Zoe caught sight of her mother's face. Aleta noticed. She arched a brow and glowed all the brighter.

Apparently, Zoe's mom fully approved of what was going on. But then, what proud mama wouldn't want her baby girl getting romantic with the most eligible man in Texas?

Still, it was common knowledge that Dax dated a lot of different women, that he showed no inclination to settle down. Aleta had to know that. Yet the gleam in her eyes seemed to hint that she heard wedding bells.

Zoe made a mental note to disabuse her of that notion the next time they had lunch together—which should be soon.

She got her mother alone for a moment after the meal. They agreed to meet for lunch Thursday.

When Zoe and Dax left to return to SA early that evening, Kira sidled up and tugged on his hand. "Goodbye, Dax."

"Goodbye, Kira. Nice to meet you."

She grinned shyly at that, revealing a new gap in front where she'd lost her first baby tooth. "I hope you come back soon."

Aleta beamed as she'd been beaming all night. "He will, honey. Very soon."

They were on the highway, headed home, when he announced in a thoroughly annoying offhanded tone, "We'll stop at the condo. You can get what you need for overnight."

She answered in a patient voice. "Dax, we need to keep at least a little perspective on this situation."

"You. Me. My bed. All night. That's the perspective I'm talking about."

"You are blowing me off."

"The last thing I'm doing is blowing you off. I want the whole night with you. Then in the morning, we can just go in to work together."

"No, we're not getting into that. I want to go to work by myself. I don't want to waltz in with you tomorrow morning and have Lin and the rest of them start thinking how sad it is. That they like me, but the writing's on the wall. Soon enough, I'll be out of there and they'll have to break in a new assistant."

"It's none of their business. Ignore them."

"Of course it's their business. They have to work with me—*and* whoever you hire when I'm gone."

"Didn't we say we weren't going to predict the future when it comes to you and me?"

"No, Dax. You said that. And I'm not predicting the future."

"Yeah, you are."

"No, I'm talking about my working relationship with my colleagues. I don't want to lose their respect because I'm just like every other assistant you ever had and can't keep my hands off the boss."

"But you *can't* keep your hands off the boss—and the boss is really happy about that."

"God, you are so smug."

That shut him up. For maybe thirty seconds. Then he sent her a conciliatory glance. "So, how about *your* bed? Just for an hour or two? Then I will get up, put my clothes on and go. You can sleep alone and drive to work all by yourself."

She reached over and touched his hand. "Thank you."

By way of an answer, he caught her fingers and raised them to his lips.

She held his gaze for a moment, spoke softly, "Weekends, we can sleep together. Whenever we don't have to go into the office the next day."

"Got it."

"And that was rude of me. I shouldn't have called you smug."

"We'll be at your place in about seven minutes. You can show me how sorry you are then."

He was as good as his word. He made beautiful love to her and then he got up and went back to his house.

Monday night, she went to him. And Tuesday, as well.

By Wednesday, yawning at her desk, she admitted to herself that some other arrangement would have to be made.

That night, he brought a suitcase to her house with the essentials and they enjoyed the luxury of falling asleep in each other's arms. The next day, they went to work in separate cars, though. And she left for the office before he did.

That was Thursday. She met her mom for lunch in a quiet Olmos Park restaurant Aleta liked.

Aleta asked about the magazine. Zoe told her how happy she was to be working there.

"We all enjoyed getting to know Dax a little better last Sunday…." Delicately, Aleta dabbed the corner of her lip with her snowy napkin.

Zoe said, "I'm glad that you invited him."

"And your sister tells me he called her Tuesday. About Donovan McRae."

"He told me he wasn't able to find out much." Zoe tasted her blackened catfish. Perfect. "McRae's at his retreat in the desert, pretty much on lockdown. Nobody knows what's up with him."

"True, Dax didn't have much information for Abilene. Still, it was thoughtful of him, kind of him, to try." Her mother sipped her glass of sauvignon blanc. "I like Dax, Zoe. I like him very much."

Zoe set her fork on the edge of her plate. "Yes, Mom. We *are* seeing each other, dating each other."

A flush stained Aleta's still-smooth cheeks. "Oh. Well. I thought so—and I'm pleased to have my guess confirmed."

"I care for him. A lot. And he cares for me. But… well, you shouldn't get your mind moving in the direction of a wedding or anything. That's not going to happen."

Aleta made a low sound, both disbelieving and slightly distressed. "But, honey, how do you know that?"

"We've talked about it. We…understand each other."

"Well, you never know what might happen in the end, though, do you? I realize he…enjoys pretty women. But then, you're special. I think he sees that. I think he knows what a prize you are."

"Mom, of course you think I'm special. You're my mother."

"I think you're special because you *are* special."

"And I love that about you. Thank you. Having a mother like you is definitely confidence-building. But my having all the confidence in the world is not going to make Dax Girard into someone he isn't."

"But…" Aleta started to say something, and then seemed to think better of it. She drew a slow breath, gave a gracious nod. "I only want you to be happy, that's all."

"And I am, Mom. Very happy. I love my job. I'm crazy about Dax. And he's crazy about me, too. I plan to live every moment to the fullest and not waste time or precious energy on second-guessing or regrets."

And Zoe did live in the moment.

In the weeks that followed, she and Dax managed to spend most nights together.

In the daytime, at work, they kept it strictly professional. It wasn't that difficult, since they both knew that when nighttime came, they would be sharing the same bed.

In September, they went to Greece for the February Spotlight. There, they relaxed the rules a little and allowed themselves to be truly together round-the-clock. It was a lovely time. They spent most of it on the world-famous island of Mykonos, enjoying the sun and sand, the jewel-blue Aegean, the laid-back, wide-open nightlife.

Ramón Esquevar took the pictures for that story. So Zoe got to meet him at last. He was kind to her, discussing their mutual love of photography with her, giving her pointers but never talking down to her.

They stayed for a week. And returned tanned and rested, only to have to work extra hard to catch up again.

Zoe loved that about her job. There was always the next trip to plan, always more to do than there were hours in the day.

On the first Monday in October, they went to the South of France for Dax's last Spotlight trip of the year. In November and December, he would use contributing editors for the corresponding publication months of April and May. The trip to France lasted five memorable days.

And then it was back home and the mad rush to get on top of the workload once again.

After business hours, Dax seemed as taken with her as ever. He wanted to be with her every chance he got. She felt the same about him. Sometimes they would make love for hours, and sometimes they would lie together in the dark, talking about any- and everything, late into the night.

She was, she realized, truly happy. Excited to get up

and face each day. And yet content, too. Her life, finally, seemed to be on-track.

Well, except for that one nagging worry, the one that moved from the back of her mind to the forefront as the weeks passed.

She hadn't had a period since the last week of July.

Chapter Thirteen

Aleta Bravo had given birth to nine children.

In her fifties now, she prided herself on her slim figure. She always said that she knew it was a false pride, that she was just one of those women who didn't gain a lot of weight with a baby—and then, without really having to work for it, got her flat stomach back again within a few months of the baby's birth.

Simple genetics, Aleta always said. She had easy pregnancies and relatively easy labors, as well.

By mid-October, when almost three months had passed since Zoe's last period, she was reasonably sure she was pregnant, that she had been since Mexico. And that she took after her mother.

Zoe's stomach remained flat. She suffered no signs of morning sickness. True, the smell of certain foods made her vaguely nauseated. Liquor, too. But that was easily handled. She stopped drinking alcohol and she avoided the foods that didn't agree with her.

She had told no one of her suspicions. And since she hadn't put on weight and never had to run for the restroom, no one seemed to guess.

Zoe had found it easy enough to ignore the obvious for all those weeks. She'd told herself she was just late. Her cycle had been knocked out of whack by the stress of the life-and-death experience in Chiapas, by all the changes in her world in recent months: her wonderful, demanding job. And her sexy lover who also happened to be her boss.

But by the third week in October, she knew that she had to face the truth. She bought a home test, a digital one with a high rating for accuracy and ease of use.

Then she waited.

For a night when Dax had an editorial to finish and didn't come home with her.

When that finally happened, on the last Tuesday in October, she took the test in her own bathroom, by herself, the next morning.

The result window read *Pregnant*.

Suddenly, she wanted to throw up, but not really from morning sickness. More from pure shock to have her months-long, nagging suspicion confirmed.

Still, the test's instructions said to retest a week later, just to make sure. And then to see a doctor for a final confirmation if the second test came out positive.

She decided to skip the second home test and cut to the chase. When she called her doctor's office, they told her they could fit her in that day, during her lunch hour. Did she want to make the appointment for then?

Did she want to? Not on your life. But she did it anyway. "Yes. Please. I'll be there."

During their morning huddle, Dax asked her if something was wrong. "You okay? You seem…I don't know, distracted."

She lied, she said everything was fine.

And that afternoon at quarter of one, she got the doctor's diagnosis.

She was officially pregnant. About twelve weeks, with a projected due date of May seventh.

Twelve weeks along. That meant she'd gotten pregnant in the rainforest, way back at the beginning. Even though they had always been careful to use a condom every single time. According to various sources—yes, she had looked it up during those weeks and weeks she was in denial—condoms were ninety-eight-percent effective in preventing pregnancy if used every single time, with zero breakage.

Wouldn't you know she'd fall in the inevitable two percent? Her mom used to joke that she only had to *look* at her dad to end up pregnant. So maybe that was just another way Zoe took after her mother.

She couldn't face going back to the office, seeing Dax, talking to him, trying to pretend her whole world hadn't just tipped on its axis—or *not* to pretend. To simply tell him what she'd finally found out for sure.

Oh, yeah. That was going to go over well. Tell the man who carried condoms with him wherever he went—and used them every time, even when his plane went down in the jungle—that he might have to revise his stance on having kids.

Uh-uh.

Not that.

No, thank you.

Not today.

Zoe went home.

Next step: notify Dax that she wouldn't be back in that day.

She considered calling HR or maybe Lin. Getting someone else to relay the message would have been so much easier than having to talk to him, to hear his voice.

To lie to him.

Or to tell him the truth.

But if she didn't talk to him personally, he would only end up calling her anyway to find out what was going on with her.

She dithered over whether a text would do it—and knew that it wouldn't. He would only call her as soon as he received it. So she made herself autodial his cell.

He answered instantly. "There you are."

"Hey."

He pretended to scold her. "I'll have you know you're half an hour late back from lunch." And then he grew concerned. "Really, though. Everything okay?"

"I'm…I think I might be coming down with something." *Like, you know, your baby?*

"You did seem a little out of it this morning."

"I'm fine, really."

"Fine?"

"Yes, that's what I said."

"So why don't I believe you?"

"Well, okay. Not *that* fine. I came on home."

"Good idea. Fever?"

"Uh…no. A killer headache. And I, well, I feel sick." She did feel sick, so she hadn't just told him a *total* lie.

"Take a Tylenol. Drink liquids. Go to bed."

"I plan to. Thanks."

"I'll be over to check on you as soon as I can get out of here."

"No!" She said it too fast—and too loud. Too late, she clapped her hand over her mouth.

"Zoe? What the hell is up with you?"

"Nothing."

"You're scaring me." His sounded gruff. And honestly concerned for her welfare.

"Sorry, really. I just…no need for both of us to get this bug." The nine-month bug. Hah!

"I'll stop by for only a few minutes. I promise not to get too close to you, no matter how you try and tempt me."

"Dax, I—"

"Go to bed. I mean it. See you soon."

And he hung up.

She went to her bedroom, shut the blinds, took off her shoes, stretched out on the bed and stared blindly at the ceiling. *Soon,* he'd said. *See you soon.*

When, exactly, was soon?

He had a key. Just as she had one to his place. She didn't really need his key. He always had staff at his house to answer the door if she should show up when he wasn't around. He'd given a key to her anyway. "I want you to have it," he'd said. "So no matter what, if you need to get in there, you can."

And she'd given him her key for the same reason.

And since he thought she was sick, he would probably just let himself in. He wouldn't want to wake her if she was getting some asleep.

She closed her eyes with a long sigh. No way would she sleep. She was too edgy, too weirded out by the whole situation.

On the other hand, it did help. To lie here in the quiet of her darkened bedroom, to let her thoughts drift away...

What seemed like a minute or two after she shut her eyes, Zoe woke up. She lay there for a moment, unmoving, surprised that she had fallen asleep after all. The bedside clock said it was now after four.

And Dax was sitting in the chair in the corner. "Hey, sleepyhead." He looked at her so fondly, a warm smile curving those lips she loved to kiss.

She sat up, raked her tangled hair back off her face. "Ugh. How long have you been here?"

"Not long. Ten minutes maybe."

"You should have woken me."

"Why? You need your sleep to get well."

She almost laughed. As if sleep was going to make everything better.

His dark brows drew together. "Zoe, what's going on?"

She stalled, rubbing at her eyes, not even caring that she was smearing her mascara.

When she finally looked at him again and saw he was still watching her, waiting for some kind of reasonable answer, she realized that she wasn't up for any more deception. She'd been lying to herself for months. And she wasn't going to lie anymore—not to herself.

And not to him.

He needed to know.

She raked her fingers through her hair a second time. "I went to the doctor on my lunch hour."

He stiffened in the chair. "My God. Is it something serious?"

"Serious enough. I'm pregnant."

It wasn't all that easy to shock Dax Girard, but her announcement had done it. His mouth dropped open. Slowly, he shut it. "That's…not possible. We used a condom. We used one every time."

She blew out a breath. "I did a little research on the effectiveness of condoms. Let me share what I learned."

"Please. Do."

"Two percent per year, Dax. With perfect, every-time use of a condom, two women in a hundred will still end up getting pregnant. As it has turned out, I'm one of those. One in fifty. I feel really special."

"And the pill? I thought you mentioned you were going on the pill, too?"

"I did say that. And I was. The way that works is you start taking the pills the first day of your period. But I never had my period. So I never started on the pills."

He considered the ramifications of that. "You mean you haven't had a period since…?"

"The week before the Chiapas trip."

"Three months." He said it in a wondering tone.

"Yeah, I know. I've been pregnant since the beginning. Maybe even since the very first time we were together, on the night of the day I got up close and personal with that boa constrictor. My doctor confirms it. He says I'm twelve weeks along."

Dax just sat there. He stared into the middle distance.

She said what she had to say. "Look, I understand, given how you feel about being a dad—which is that you don't want to be one, ever—and given that you've always taken precautions to protect against pregnancy… well, given all that, I get that you might doubt me, doubt my word that this is your baby and—"

"Don't." He glared at her. "Do not put words in my mouth. I don't doubt you. I know you. I know you wouldn't lie about something like this. I know it's... mine. Now, I'm just trying to process, okay? I'm acting like a jerk and I realize that. It's only... It's a big surprise, that's all."

She wrapped her arms around herself, sucked in a slow breath. "Yes. All right. I get that. I do."

"You want this baby."

It wasn't a question, but she answered him as if it had been. "The timing is not so great, I know. But yeah. I want this baby. I'm going to have this baby, be...this baby's mom."

He focused directly on her then. For the longest time. He sat there in the chair across the rug from her and he studied her. Was he judging her and finding her a liar, in spite of what he'd said a few moments before?

Or did he actually understand and sympathize?

She wished she knew.

He got up. She watched him as he came to her. He stood above her, touched her upturned face with a gentle hand, brushed a curl of hair back from her forehead, tracing the line of it, along her temple, down her cheek.

She searched his eyes, whispered, "Dax. What...?"

He sat down beside her and put his arm around her, gathering her near to him.

She knew such sweet relief then, just to feel his sheltering touch. To discover that he wasn't going to hate her, to blame her. She sagged against him.

He guided her head down onto his shoulder. "It's all going to work out. Don't worry. It will be fine."

She gave a sad little chuckle. "*I* say I'm fine. *You*

say it will be fine. I guess that's what people do in a situation like this."

"Guess so." He tipped her chin up so she met his eyes again. His gaze was so tender. So fond. And very much present, very much with her in that quiet bedroom. The faraway look was gone. "It could be a lot worse. You could be some stranger. Or someone boring. But I know you to the core of you. And you are smart and beautiful and strong. And always exciting to me, even now, when you look so worried, so sad."

His words did warm her. She gave him a wobbly smile. "I'm so relieved at how you're taking this."

He squeezed her shoulder in reassurance. "It's going to be—"

She made a low sound. "Fine?"

"Yeah. Yeah, it is." He kissed her temple. "I'm thirty-five years old," he said.

"Right. Just ancient. I realize that."

"I've been with a lot of women."

"No need to rub it in."

"May I finish?"

"Oops. Sorry. Yes."

"There's never been any woman in my life like you. You joke about being one in fifty, being special. To me it's no joke. You *are* special, Zoe."

"Oh, Dax." She swallowed down the tightness in her throat. "Please don't make me cry, okay? I'm too exhausted for a crying jag right now."

"Just don't worry. Please. I will take care of you and the baby. We'll get married and—"

She jumped back as if he'd slapped her. "What did you say? Tell me you didn't just say that."

He frowned, puzzled. "What? What did I do?"

"I could have sworn you just mentioned marriage."

"Well." He actually looked kind of pleased with himself. "Yeah. Yeah, I did."

"But…" She struggled to find the words. "You don't want to get married. You're never getting married again, remember?"

He frowned. And then he stood, paced to the chair where he'd been sitting when she woke up, and turned on his heel to face her again. "That was before."

"Before…what?"

"Before you and me. And the baby. Everything's different now. We'll get married. It will work out. You'll see."

She was shaking her head. "Dax, it's not what you want. You know it. I know it. There's no reason to go getting into something you don't even want, especially something as important as marriage."

He dropped into the chair. Bracing his elbows on his spread knees, he leaned toward her, his expression intent. "You're doing it again. Putting words in my mouth."

"Words *you* said and said very clearly."

"That was three months ago. Everything's changed now."

"You said *never,* Dax. You said you would never get married and you would never have children. You were very sure about it. Up-front, you know? Honest. I respected that."

"Well, and guess what? I was wrong. I'm willing to admit that, willing to move on from that. Is there some reason *you* can't move on, too?"

She thought about the things he'd revealed to her, when it was just the two of them alone in the jungle, with only each other to turn to. And she told him, softly, "I won't, Dax. I won't be Nora all over again."

He swore. "You're not. I am very well aware that you're not. I never so much as hinted that you're like Nora in any way."

"And I *won't* be like Nora. I'm not going to...trap you into something you didn't sign on for."

"I don't think you're trapping me."

"Maybe not. But *I* would feel like I was trapping you."

"So get over it." He growled the words.

She refused to back down on this. "It's just not that simple."

"Because you're making it complicated."

"No, I'm not. No more complicated that it actually is." She held his eyes, willed him to listen, to look into his own heart. "Don't you see? The baby, well, it's happening. You're going to have to deal with that. As a man. As a future father. And I deeply admire you for stepping right up, for being such a stand-up guy about this when we both know this is exactly what was *not* supposed to happen. Yes, I agree that a two-parent home is the ideal. But it's by no means the only way for a child to get the love and guidance needed in life. Matt and Corrine had Kira without getting married. They were excellent coparents for five years. They worked together for Kira's sake, but they kept their lives separate. In the end, they decided to marry, yes. But they were doing a terrific job without being husband and wife. I think we can do a good job, too. I really do. There's absolutely no reason we have to—"

"There is every reason." His voice was hard. "Why won't you believe me when I tell you that you are not, and never could be, another Nora to me? That was more than a decade ago. Nora is nothing like you. And I'm a different man now."

"But still a man who doesn't want to get married, a man who is having a child he didn't sign on for. Uh-uh. It's not right. Marriage is not what you want, not what you ever wanted. You were crystal clear about that. There is no reason to go there."

"There is every reason."

"I'm sorry. I don't agree. I simply don't."

He stared across the sudden chasm between them, tension rolling off him in waves. She knew he was barely holding back from leaping up, grabbing her by the shoulders and trying to shake some sense into her—*his* kind of sense.

Finally, in a deadly soft voice, he said, "It doesn't matter what I do, does it? There is nothing I can say. You've got it all worked out in your mind and that is how it's going to be." He rose to his feet.

She saw in his eyes that he was leaving. "Dax, please. Can't we just take a deep breath here? Can't we just back off on this? It doesn't all have to be worked out tonight."

He was not appeased. "But it is worked out, isn't it? As far as *you're* concerned anyway. And when it comes to us, you run the show. I'm lucky to get to go along for the ride."

"Dax, that's not fair."

"Maybe not, but it's the truth. We are perfect for each other. We understand each other. We love the same things. You're as crazy for me as I am for you. The sex is amazing. *And* you happen to be having my baby. But none of that matters. Because you've made up your mind that you're *not* going to marry me. You know what's right for me and you're going to see that I get it—whether it's what I want or not. End of story. All she wrote."

She longed to tell him he was wrong, that he had judged her too harshly. But how could she say that when she *had* made up her mind and she *wasn't* going to marry him? All the things he had just mentioned were true. They had a lot in common. In many ways, they were very right for each other. But not when it came to marriage and children. Because she wanted them. And he didn't.

Zoe pulled her shoulders back and faced him squarely. "No, I'm not going to marry you."

He had that look again—like he wanted to shake her. Or maybe strangle her.

Instead, without another word, he turned and left her. She heard him in the entryway, pulling the front door wide. He closed it quietly behind him, but she winced at the faint sound nonetheless.

Chapter Fourteen

All evening, Zoe kept hoping he'd call—or show up at her door again.

But he didn't.

And she didn't call him.

She decided that maybe it was better to leave it alone for a while. Give him time. Give *her* time. To get used to the idea that there was going to be a baby in their lives, to start coming to grips with the big changes the baby would bring.

In the morning, she considered calling in sick, but she wasn't sick. She was perfectly healthy. Tired, yes, but certainly capable of going in to work.

And moping around the condo didn't hold much appeal. At work, there would be, as always, way too much to do. And that would be wonderful. It would help her keep her mind off her worries.

Yes, her biggest worry of all would be showing up

about a half hour after she got there. Dealing with Dax right now was almost certain to be...uncomfortable. He would probably find interesting ways to make her miserable, to try to bully her into letting him do the "right thing," which they both knew was absolutely the wrong thing for him.

But she could handle Dax. Plus, calling in sick might give him an excuse to start thinking about getting rid of her. It was a distinct possibility that he might not want her working for him anymore, now that she was having his baby. Now that they were so completely on the outs over what to do about it.

If he fired her, so be it. She'd pick up the pieces and move on. But no way was she showing him weakness; no way would she give him any reason to start thinking that she couldn't deal with working for him now.

She loved her job and she was holding on to it until the bitter end, until he told her to leave or they carried her out on a stretcher, far gone in labor—and not even then, if she could help it.

Her plan was to take six weeks' pregnancy leave and then to come back.

So she ate a protein-rich breakfast, piled on the concealer to cover the dark circles under her eyes and went to work.

Dax fully expected Zoe to take a day off. Even so furious at her he couldn't see straight, he realized that she was beat, that she needed a little time to herself.

He was even a little worried she might decide to give notice. Now he'd finally found the perfect assistant, the last thing he wanted was to lose her too soon.

No, he had a right to several more months of her excellent personal services before it became necessary to promote her to keep some other rag from stealing her away.

Even if she *was* having his baby and being ridiculously obstinate about how to deal with that.

Not to mention insulting. He was a decade older than she was, yet sometimes she treated him like an overgrown boy. She had cut him to the core the previous evening. And he wasn't going to forgive her until she came to her senses and admitted how wrong she had been.

A little groveling, too. That was definitely in order. A little begging him to forgive her for judging him so wrongly. That would be nice.

But his frustrated fury at her didn't mean he was willing to get along without her at the office. No. Not that. Not until he absolutely had to.

He fully expected her to take the day off, regroup and come back in Friday, refreshed and ready to see to his every need—in a professional sense at least.

And as to her sincere apology and inevitable agreement that they really should get married? He accepted that she was a proud woman, too proud, really, for her own good. And he understood that it might take her a few days to come to her senses about their future.

A few days would still be too long. But he was willing to wait if she needed the time to face reality.

Shocked the hell out of him when the elevator doors slid open and there she was, his coffee in her outstretched hand. Wearing a snug pink blouse and skirt to match, she was the female equivalent of strawberry ice cream. She made him want to lick her right up.

Three months along. It didn't seem possible. Her belly was as slim and tight as it had ever been.

"Good morning, Dax." She smiled. That adorable dimple tucked itself temptingly into her pink cheek.

He said nothing. He took the coffee, removed the lid, sniffed it, sipped it, put the lid back on. And went into his office and shut the door.

Fifteen minutes later, he called her in for the huddle. As always, they kept it strictly business. Yeah, okay. He might have tossed her a glowering glance or two.

But he got nothing back but cheerful smiles and direct responses to his questions. For her, it was business as usual. Zoe was on the job and sharp and efficient as ever.

The whole day went by and she gave zero indication that she needed to see him alone, to explain to him how off-base she had been, to tell him she only wanted his forgiveness—and his ring on her finger.

Didn't she get it? She only had to make it clear that she was very, very sorry, and he would make love to her all night long. Then in the morning, he would get her an enormous diamond. A real diamond bigger than the fake one she'd bought back when she was pretending to be engaged to the nonexistent Johnny.

They would tell her family together. And sometime in the next few weeks, they would get married.

He was tired of going back and forth to that little condo of hers anyway. He was ready to have her at his house all the time, to be able to take her anywhere and proudly introduce her as his wife.

As soon as she quit being stubborn about this, they could get on with their lives.

But Zoe never said she was sorry.

Friday went by. And the weekend. And the next week. And the week after that.

She came to work every day with a smile on her face. She looked great. Her stomach stayed flat.

He started to worry that maybe she had lost the baby. Lost *their* baby and never said a word to him.

Could that be possible? Was he cursed? Did he bring nothing but heartache to the women who cared for him?

First Nora and now Zoe, carrying his baby.

And then losing it.

He began to see things differently, to wonder if maybe *he* was in the wrong. Wrong to let this drag on like this, with this distance he hated between them, when Zoe was carrying his child—or had lost his child—and needed him to be with her. Needed him to support her the way a man is meant to support the woman who matters to him.

He saw that *he* was the stubborn one, the one with all the foolish pride.

And what had his pride gotten him but loneliness? He hated not being with her after the workday was through, hated how empty his giant house seemed without her, hated how he even missed her dinky little condo, as long as he was in it with her.

But they had a kind of routine established at that point, a routine that she showed no inclination to change. Through the day, they were together in a strictly professional sense. And neither mentioned the baby, or their relationship as a man and a woman—their *lack* of a relationship lately.

It had become a habit so quickly, to be miserable and pretend he wasn't, to keep it all bottled up inside, to tell himself constantly that she had to come to him. That she *would* come to him.

But she never did. It wasn't happening as he'd expected and he needed to do something about that.

Soon. Very soon.

It had all…gotten away from him somehow. Suddenly, Thanksgiving was almost upon them. The holidays loomed just around the corner.

His housekeeper was already making plans to put up the giant tree in the foyer, in the curve of the grand staircase. And the head groundskeeper had come to him the week before to get his approval on the outdoor Christmas light display.

As a rule, Dax didn't take a lot of interest in the holidays. Growing up without a mother or siblings, with a dad who sometimes worked on Christmas Day, the holidays had never felt all that special or meaningful to him.

But he discovered that this year, he wanted them to be special. And meaningful. He wanted to share them with Zoe.

Starting with Thanksgiving.

Zoe would probably go to her family's ranch for Thanksgiving, wouldn't she? If they got back together before then, he could go, too. He would like that. He enjoyed her family. They were smart, interesting people.

Not that it really mattered to him where they went, as long as they went there together.…

On a lonely Wednesday night, a week and a day before Thanksgiving, he stood at one of the tall front windows in his formal living room. He sipped good Scotch, thought about how three Sundays had passed since it all blew apart. Had she been to the ranch for Sunday dinner in those weeks? Had any of her siblings or Aleta or Davis asked about him, wondered why he wasn't with her?

This was getting beyond ridiculous. It had to stop. Being without her made him feel all wrong inside his own skin.

At least in the daytime, five days a week, he got to see her, talk to her. Be near her, if not *with* her. Nights, like tonight, though, it got bad. The empty house echoed.

Action was called for, he thought for the umpteenth time. He needed to go after her.

And he *would* go after her.

Soon.

Zoe stood at the front window in her cozy living room, her hand resting on the slight curve of her belly, and stared out at the little patch of lawn in front of her condo. The condo association was talking about ripping out that tiny patch, putting in xeriscape to conserve precious water. That would probably happen in the spring. In the meantime, she had the small square of currently winter-brown grass.

Maybe sometime in the next couple of weeks, she would get over to one of the local home-improvement centers and pick up a couple of wire reindeer, the ones with little gold lights and moving parts—heads that went from side to side, or up and down, as if they were cropping the soon-to-be nonexistent grass.

Definitely. Reindeer on her square of lawn. That would be festive.

And cheerful, as well.

Lately, she needed every bit of cheer she could get. She kept up a good front at the office. But at home, well, it was too easy to get feeling grim.

Idly, she stroked the barely-there roundness of her

tummy. It was happening, finally. She was starting to get an actual stomach. The baby was making her—or his—presence known. About time, too. She would hit the four-month mark the first week in December.

December.

It would be there before she knew it. December—and Christmas without Dax.

Why did that make her feel desolate? Last year, she hadn't even *known* the guy.

But then, she'd had to go and fall hopelessly in love with him. Now Christmas without him seemed as awful to contemplate as Thanksgiving was going to be.

She needed to go to him, try and work it out with him, to reach some kind of peace and understanding with him. It couldn't go on forever this way, could it?

The really sad and scary thing was that she feared it actually could.

She was acting like a total coward and she knew it. She dreaded facing him, dreaded the idea of trying again, to make him see that marriage wasn't any answer. Not for them. That she just couldn't do that to him.

And really, it was kind of funny how even though she hadn't worked up the guts to confront Dax again, she now had no qualms about facing down her family—including her dad.

She had become beyond brave and take-charge when it came to them. Just the previous Sunday she'd gone to dinner at Bravo Ridge.

And she had told them all about the baby.

Of course, they'd all wanted to know where Dax was.

She barely got in the door before Ash, her oldest brother, said, "Sorry Dax couldn't make it."

She went straight for the flat-out truth. "Well, since we're only speaking at the office nowadays, I saw no reason to invite him."

Ash put his hand on her shoulder. "Sometimes love is…difficult."

A small, sad laugh escaped her. "Tell me about it."

"You'll work it out, I know you will."

"Thanks, Ash. I hope you're right."

Tessa, Ash's wife, stood beside him, holding their new baby, David Patrick, who had been born just a couple of weeks before. Zoe asked if she might hold the tiny boy.

"Of course." Tessa laid him in Zoe's waiting arms. He scrunched up his tiny nose at her and wiggled his plump, perfect fists.

"So beautiful," Zoe whispered.

"Yes," Tessa agreed in the doting, tender voice of a brand-new mother. "He is."

Before they sat down to eat, Aleta *and* Abilene both asked after Dax. Zoe told them pretty much what she'd told Ash.

They each started reassuring her like mad, that it would all work out, that everything would be fine.

She thanked them. And hugged them. And told them she loved them in a tone that made it clear she wanted to leave it at that—for the time being anyway.

At the table, as soon as everyone was served the main course, she tapped her spoon against her water glass.

"Everyone, I have an announcement I'd like to make."

They all stopped eating and looked at her. Even the children stared. She hesitated. Was it appropriate, to say what she was about to say in front of the little ones?

Yes, she decided. It should be all right. Kira was the

oldest, at six, and still too young to really get what was going on. Plus, lots of kids were raised in single-parent homes. Kira herself had lived between her dad's house and her mom's until just the past January.

So Zoe went ahead and shared her big news. "I'm pregnant. Fifteen weeks along." They all blinked in unison. Actually, the sight was kind of comical. "I know, I'm hardly showing." She gave her mom a fond smile. "I guess I take after our mother that way. The baby is Dax's. Yes, he's offered to marry me. I turned him down. I just wanted you all to know that I love you and appreciate you. And you all need to get used to the idea that this is happening." She looked squarely at her dad. "And you all are not, under any circumstances, to interfere. I am having a baby. I am going to keep it. And I am *not* getting married." She had said *you all,* but she continued to stare only at her dad. "This is not a screwup, not some flaky, free-spirit, irresponsible act. We took precautions and it happened anyway. And now, well, I'm happy about it. I really am. I am quite capable of raising my child and it is my choice to do so. And if any of you have issues with my choice, I would appreciate it if you'd get them out in the open now, so we can deal with them and move on."

Marnie was the first to speak. "Zoe, this is wonderful news. I know you're going to be an excellent mom."

"I'll second that," said Corrine. "You will do great. And we're all here to help in any way we can."

And then her dad said, "What can I tell you, Zoe? I think you're capable of tackling just about any task you set your mind to. I love you and I want only the best for you. Congratulations."

Zoe peered at him intently, looking for a catch. But it didn't appear that there was one.

Her mom smiled her most loving smile. "We support you, honey. And we are right here whenever you need us."

"Yes, we are." Her dad spoke roughly, with considerable emotion. Zoe could see the love in his green eyes. And more. She saw admiration in his gaze, as well. And that meant so much.

Now, three evenings later, standing at her front window, planning to put some lighted wire reindeer on her tiny square of lawn, Zoe only wished that dealing with Dax could be one half as simple as breaking the news to her family had been.

The next day, Thursday, Dax called Aleta.

He asked her if he might have a word with her and Davis.

She invited him over for dinner that night.

Zoe's parents were warm and welcoming. Aleta hugged him. Davis shook his hand.

Gingerly, once they sat down to eat, he tried to feel them out, to discover before he said too much if Zoe might have already told them about the baby.

"I...don't know if you were aware that Zoe and I have been having some problems lately."

Aleta smiled her dazzling smile. "Last Sunday, she told us all that you two are having a baby. *And* that you have asked her to marry you and she turned you down. Also, she mentioned to me that you two are only speaking when you're at the office."

She hasn't lost the baby. The baby—our baby—*is all right.*

Sweet relief poured through him at the news. Dax set down his fork. "I had a feeling you knew *something*. I just wasn't sure how much."

Davis cut right to the heart of the matter. "You're hoping we can help you change her mind, is that it?"

Gratitude warmed him—for their kindness. For their understanding. "I am, yes. I sincerely want to marry your daughter, and to…be a real dad to our child."

Davis chuckled then.

Dax frowned. It hardly seemed a chuckle-worthy moment to him. "What?"

The older man shook his head. "Sorry, son. It's not that we don't want the same things for you—and for Zoe, and especially for our grandchild."

"We do," Aleta chimed in with feeling. "Very much."

Davis said, "We're on your side, believe me."

"But she made us promise—" Aleta shared a tender glance with her husband "—not to interfere."

Davis told him, "I think if you want our daughter, if you *really* want her, you're going to have to start talking to her. You're going to have to find a way to get past whatever's come between you."

"And…I should do this how?"

Davis and Aleta shared another fond look. And then Davis said, "If I had a clue, I would tell you. But then again, is that really my job? I don't think so. I think it's yours, Dax. I think you've got some serious convincing to do. I wish you all the best with that. I hope you succeed. I think you and my little girl are good together. I would love to have you in the family. But I can't make that happen. Only *you* can—you and Zoe, together."

The next morning, when Dax got off the elevator at *Great Escapes,* Zoe was there, as she was every morning, sitting behind her desk, her red hair shining, so pretty it almost hurt to look at her.

He thought about holding her. He thought about kissing her. He thought about the way the two of them used to stay awake half the night, whispering to each other in the dark.

She glanced up from her computer monitor and gave him a cool smile. "Good morning, Dax."

He smiled back, a *real* smile. "Zoe."

She looked slightly shocked, but then she stood and handed him his coffee. "Here you go."

He took off the lid and sipped, forgoing for once the big pretence of sniffing it first. He asked, really hoping for an answer, "How are you feeling?"

"I'm doing well."

"The baby?"

She stiffened and her eyes narrowed. He wasn't surprised. After all, he was blatantly breaking the rules, to bring up the baby here, at the office, where they were supposed to keep it strictly professional.

Well, screw the rules. The baby was more important than any damn rule.

After a few strained seconds, she visibly relaxed. Her hand slipped down to rest on her stomach, and for the first time, he thought he detected a slight roundness there.

Something strange moved through him at the sight. This really was happening. To her. To him.

A new life was coming. He would have another chance to step up and be the dad he hadn't known how to be with his first child, the child lost before she had ever had a chance to live.

He saw it all now. Saw that this moment was everything. This was his chance to begin to make things right. He was not going to blow it.

"The baby is fine," she said softly. "No worries."

"Good. I'm glad. I *was* worried."

A wobbly smile tried to form on her lips. She didn't let it. "Well, don't be. I'm all right and the baby is, too." She sat back down at her desk, put her hands on the keyboard, started typing again—and then stopped. She waited. And then finally, when he didn't go away, she dropped her hands to her lap and slanted him a dismissing look. "Anything else?"

"Come into my office, please. Come in now."

Her heart going like a trip-hammer and her stomach suddenly roiling, Zoe went through the door behind Dax.

When they were both in the room, he stopped, reached around her and pushed the door shut. Then he just stood there, looking at her.

She hitched up her chin, forced herself to meet those wonderful dark eyes. "Yes? What is it?"

"I love you. You know that, right?"

It stole all the breath from her body, to hear him say it right out like that. "I…" She put her hands to her cheeks, which were flaming hot. Her palms, on the other hand, were like ice.

"Do you know that, Zoe?"

She dropped her hands, made herself nod, somehow managed to speak around the log that had lodged itself in her throat. "I…yes. I know. I do know."

"And I do want to marry you. I want it with all my heart. I want you. And I want our baby."

She couldn't keep looking at him. He was such a gorgeous man and he held her heart in his big, strong hands. She turned away, put her arms around herself, stared at a grouping of framed *Great Escapes* covers on the far wall.

He stepped closer behind her. Although he had the grace to not touch her, she could feel him there. Faintly, the wonderful, tempting scent of him teased at her.

He said so quietly, "You don't believe me. You don't believe I really do want to marry you."

She still couldn't turn to him. Sharply, she shook her head.

"Well, all right," he said, still quietly. And tenderly, too. "So what is it? What do you need from me? What will make you know that I'm telling you the truth?"

She turned to him then. "Oh, Dax…" But he was too close. He made her want to forget her doubts, to throw herself into his arms, to let him hold her, let him tell her again that he loved her.

He whispered her name. "Zoe…"

She made herself step back before her need for him got the better of her. "It's only that I… Well, how can I believe you?"

Quietly, he answered. "Because I say it. Because I mean it. Because you know me and you know that I'm not a liar."

"But…everything comes so easily to you, Dax. You have it all and…it all simply comes to you. Money, beautiful things. Any woman you could possibly want. They chase you until you let them catch you. And you turn them away when you're tired of them. You do it kindly. Gently. But you do it. And then you wait for the next hopeful, pretty young thing to drop into your life. For you, Dax, the world is a banquet. You've never in your life been…hungry."

"But I have been hungry, Zoe. I'm hungry now. For you. Only you." His eyes made promises. And his voice was dark and deep as the Mexican rainforest in the middle of the night.

Oh, she did want to believe him. More than to draw her next breath, she wanted to believe him. But she just couldn't take that kind of chance. She had more than herself to think about now. "Three weeks, Dax. Since I said no when you proposed. Three weeks and you've barely spoken to me. It's not encouraging, you know?"

He swore, whirled on his heel, took two brisk steps away—and then turned back. "Look, I've been an ass and I get that I have. At first, I was waiting for you…to come around, see things my way. It took me a while— too long, I see that now—to admit that waiting for you to see the light wasn't working, not even close. I'm not as good as I should be at loving you. I'm new at this. But when I set my mind on a course, I learn fast."

"Oh, I know you do. I love that about you." She spoke with all the passion in her yearning heart.

"Zoe…" He reached out his arms.

She put up a hand. "No. Stop. Oh, Dax, can't you see? It's all just more proof of how you are. So full of grace. So effortless. You don't have to struggle, to fight, to… stick it out. In that, you're like I was before I realized I needed to change a few things. When it gets tedious or difficult, you just walk away."

"I'm not walking away. I swear it. There has only been you since the jungle. Since before then. There's been no one else since I ended it with Faye. I'm sticking by you—with you—no matter how rough it gets."

"In the long-run? Oh, I don't think so."

He stood there, three steps and a thousand miles away. "Words just aren't cutting it, are they? Words aren't enough."

She pressed her lips together, wrapped her arms tightly around her churning stomach and shook her head.

He spoke again. "Then I guess I need to figure out a way to show you. To make you see that I'm ready, Zoe. That I can be more than just the man you want. That I'm the kind of man you need."

The rest of the day went by. And Friday.

Zoe and Dax were cordial colleagues at the office. They went their separate ways at night.

The weekend came.

And it went.

And the next week was a short week at the office.

Thursday was Thanksgiving. Zoe went to Bravo Ridge at eight in the morning and helped in the kitchen, together with the other women of her family. It was a good day. Brimming with love and family laughter. She told herself it was enough, to have reached some sort of peace with Dax, to have her family around her.

But she did miss him. So much. She tried not to hope that he'd meant what he said the week before in his office, about proving to her that he truly was ready to settle down. She tried simply to be in the moment and to be thankful for what she *did* have. For her job, which she looked forward to every day. For her family, who loved and supported her. For Dax's love, whether it was destined to last…or not.

And for the child who grew within her.

For all of the important things, Zoe was grateful on Thanksgiving Day.

On Friday, Zoe, Abilene, their mom, Corrine and Marnie met at Corrine's house at 4:00 a.m. They went shopping, did Black Friday in style.

To the endless, festive loops of carols in every store, they shopped till they dropped—with a long break for a leisurely all-girls lunch around noon.

Saturday, she met Lin and some of her other coworkers at the office. They decorated every available surface. They tacked up garland and put up three trees: one by the elevator, another in the far corner at the window overlooking a major intersection outside and the third in the main conference room.

On the way home in the afternoon, she stopped at Lowe's and bought those two light-strung wire reindeer she'd had her eye on. She put them out on her patch of lawn, plugged them into a timer switch on the front step, and then went inside and put up her tree.

Sunday, she went to church with Corrine and Matt. After the service, they collected the girls from the church nursery and went back to Corrine and Matt's house for lunch. She admired Corrine's tree and the gorgeous nativity scene on the mantel. After lunch, she held little Kathleen and played Candy Land with Kira.

She left Matt's at around four.

Corrine hugged her goodbye. "Remember, if you want to talk or hang out, or just need a little support— anytime—I'm here, you only have to say the word."

Zoe thanked her and said she might be taking her up on her offer one of these days soon.

"Whenever. Just let me know."

Zoe drove home in a kind of haze of family feeling. Even without Dax at her side, it had been such a great weekend. Christmas was coming and the holiday season always lifted her spirits, brought her focus around to the happy things, made her feel good about the world and her own place in it.

But then she turned the corner on her block and

caught sight of her building—or more specifically, of the little square of lawn in front of her condo.

What in the…?

No. It wasn't possible.

She blinked, looked again.

And found it was real. It was there.

Sharing the space with her two festive wire reindeer was a yellow tent identical to the one she and Dax had shared in the jungle.

Chapter Fifteen

Dax sat in a camp chair in front of the tent, wearing hiking boots, jeans and a lightweight outdoor jacket. He was talking to Genevra Obermier, president of the condo association for the complex.

He waved as Zoe, gaping, drove past.

Genevra waved, too.

Zoe kept going. She pulled into the garage entrance and furiously punched the code into the keypad mounted there. When the steel door rolled up, she zipped in much too fast and squealed to a stop in her own numbered reserved space.

She slammed the door when she got out—childish behavior, yes, and she knew it. But she did it anyway.

In her condo, everything was as she'd left it. She turned on the tree lights and sat on the sofa and wondered why the sight of that yellow tent had made her want to cry.

It seemed…beyond wrong for him to do that. To show up where she lived with a yellow tent—a tent that somehow exemplified all they'd been through, all they'd survived.

Like a blade to the heart, she remembered it all. Eight days of hell.

And at the same time, at least in those final few days when Dax was over his fever and they were truly together, of heaven on earth.

The doorbell rang. It would be Dax, no doubt, ready to explain why he was camped out on her lawn in that damn tent that brought back way too many memories, every one of them difficult, painful—and yet, simultaneously, so achingly, gloriously sweet.

She jumped up, stalked to the door and threw it back, ready to tell him in no uncertain terms to fold up that damn tent and get it the hell off her property.

But it wasn't Dax. It was Mrs. Obermier. Zoe forced a smile. "Genevra. Hello."

"Zoe, I wonder if I might have a word?" She took off her pointy-framed pink glasses with the little rhinestone flowers and let them hang against her flat bosom by their color-coordinated fuzzy pink cord.

Dax was still there, down the front step, in that camp chair. He waved at her again.

She studiously ignored him. She would deal with him in a few minutes. She focused another tight smile on Genevra. "Coffee?"

"I would love some."

Zoe led the older woman to the kitchen. With the pod system Zoe had bought a few months back, it only took couple of minutes to brew a cup. "Milk or sugar?"

"Both would be perfect. Thank you."

Zoe got the sugar down from the cupboard and put

some milk in a small pitcher. She slid into the chair opposite Genevra and waited while the older woman stirred in a drop of milk and a very large amount of sugar.

Finally, Genevra sipped. "Delicious. Just excellent. Now, about Dax…"

Dax. Already on a first-name basis, were they? Well, in this case, Dax's irresistible charm would get him nowhere. Genevra was a real stickler when it came to community rules. And pitching a tent on the grounds was not in the rule book.

"It's all right, Genevra. I promise you. I was just going out to tell him he has to leave."

"Well, yes. I understand that. Dax said you would try to get rid of him."

"Uh. He did?"

Genevra beamed. "Yes. And please, if you could only let him remain there for a week or two…?"

"Excuse me? A *week* or two?"

"Yes, that would be so helpful."

"It would?"

"So *very* helpful. He's paid some large fees to camp out there next to those so-festive reindeer of yours. Paid in advance." Genevra sipped, leaned closer, pitched her voice to a confidential level. "Enormous fees. And you know how we've been discussing that new wing on the clubhouse? And the new weight room, the necessary pool repairs?"

About then, it all came blindingly clear. "He's paid you to let him pitch a tent on *my* lawn."

"He's paid the *fees* he intends to incur, Zoe. In advance. With a generous extra bonus thrown in. To instill goodwill."

Zoe repeated, blankly, "Goodwill."

Genevra sipped and nodded. "I know it's an imposition. And I have no idea what the appeal could be for him to suddenly decide to live in a tent outside our complex. He's very wealthy, as you know."

"I do, yes."

"What's that they say? The rich are different."

"Yes, well. I guess they are."

"And it will mean so much to the complex, to all of us, to allow him to indulge his odd little whim. Sometimes the individual must be inconvenienced for the good of the whole. You can see that, I'm sure."

What Zoe saw was the counterproductiveness of getting all up on Genevra, who only wanted the most she could get for the condo association. "Yes, all right. I do see what you're telling me."

"You'll allow him to stay, then? You won't insist that he leave?"

What could she say? "I promise, no matter what happens as far as him staying out there in that tent, that I'll get his word he'll let the association keep the money he's paid." She knew him well enough to know he wouldn't take the money back anyway. And it wasn't as if he was short on funds or anything. "How's that?"

"Thank you, Zoe. It's for the good of us all. You know that."

Genevra left a few minutes later.

And once she was gone, Zoe found she didn't have the heart to go outside. She didn't want to confront Dax, didn't want to get into it over what he thought he was up to.

So she didn't. She left him alone. If he wanted to sit out there in a tent for two weeks, so be it. Let him sit.

She felt so tired suddenly. She took a nap.

It was dark when she woke. For a moment, still

groggy with sleep, she lay there, thinking about Dax. Wondering if he would still be there on her lawn the next time she looked out the front window.

Strangely, she wasn't sure now, whether she was angry at him for this ridiculous display of…only God knew what.

Or surprisingly hopeful, oddly moved.

She got up and went out to the living room. Her tree looked magical, the tiny lights shining in the dark. She couldn't resist sidling up to the window and peeking out.

The tent was still there, light glowing from within, Dax's shadow outlined in there, faintly. The wire reindeer, set on a timer, were on. They lit up the darkness, one turning its head from side to side, the other up and down, as if cropping the brown grass.

Even when he turned off his lantern in there, the reindeer would still be shining bright. He might have trouble sleeping.

But she wasn't going to think about that.

If he had trouble sleeping, he could just go home to his enormous mansion where his extensive staff was waiting to see to his every need.

She turned from the window and went to the kitchen and made herself some dinner. Yes, she thought of taking something out to Dax, too.

But she resisted such a move.

No, she would do precisely nothing. She wouldn't make him more comfortable. She wouldn't try to get him to leave. If Dax had a point to make, he could just go ahead and make it.

In the morning, the tent was still there. When she looked out the window, Dax was sitting in the camp chair, drinking coffee from a Starbucks cup, an open laptop on his lap.

She ate breakfast; she showered and dressed and went to work. Her cell rang as she was firing up her computer.

"Good morning, Zoe."

"How are you, Dax? Sleep well?"

"Great. Listen, I won't be coming into the office for a while."

"Oh? How long?"

"I haven't decided yet."

"I see."

"Reach me here, at my cell. And forward my calls."

"Well, Dax. You're the boss."

"Yes, I am. I'm here if you need me. All you have to do is call." He hung up while she was still trying to decide what to say next.

Zoe started work. About twenty minutes after he usually came in, he called again. They did the huddle on the phone.

She went back to work.

The day went by. She forwarded a large number of calls to him. She had no idea how he dealt with them, but no one ever called back to say they couldn't reach him, so she assumed he must be handling it all well enough.

She and Lin went to lunch.

Lin said Dax had called her and told her he was camping out at Zoe's place. "In an actual tent," Lin added, disbelieving. "Is that true?"

"Oh, yes. It's true."

"Has he gone crazy?"

Zoe decided not to voice an opinion on that one. "I have no idea."

Lin shrugged. "They say the rich are different."

"That's exactly what the president of my condo association said."

Lin chuckled. "I never really understood *how* different until today."

Dax was still there, in the camp chair with the reindeer and his tent, when Zoe got home. He waved at her as she drove past.

She did not wave back.

Genevra dropped in to thank her for letting Dax stay and thus guaranteeing that the association would get to keep the piles of money he'd paid them. She said he was using the pool house shower to clean up—for an extra, very generous fee. And that a black limousine came and went with food and any other items he might need.

"Has he always been an eccentric?" Genevra asked.

Zoe shook her head. "No, not really. Not until this."

"It would be interesting to know what he's up to...."

Zoe arched an eyebrow. "I'm sure it will all become clear, as soon as he's ready to explain himself."

But Dax didn't explain himself. And Zoe didn't approach him. Tuesday went by as Monday had. And Wednesday. And the rest of the week.

Reporters started showing up. Someone in the condo association must have told someone else that the famous adventurer and magazine publisher Dax Girard had lost his mind and pitched a tent outside one of the units. Thursday, when Zoe got home from the office, there were six of them, taking pictures, asking him questions.

She went inside and spied on him through the front window. He must have been his usual incredibly charming self, because after an hour or so, they left him alone.

The next morning, he made the third page of the paper. And one of the interviews ended up on YouTube. He joked and laughed and said that you never knew where you might find your ultimate *Great Escape.*

Surprisingly, things went well enough at work. He had his minions at the mansion bring him certain software for his laptop and he did the meetings with that, videoconferencing while sitting in his camp chair next to her reindeer.

The weekend came—the first weekend in December. Dax remained in his camp in front of her condo.

Friday night, she couldn't stand leaving him out there with all those bright reindeer lights keeping him awake the whole night long. Before she went to bed, she turned them off.

Saturday, Zoe did more Christmas shopping. Again, that night, she turned off the reindeer when she went to bed. Sunday, she went to Bravo Ridge early, to help decorate the big ranch house for the holidays. She stayed for the usual afternoon dinner.

When she got home, Dax was still there. As he was Monday. And Tuesday and Wednesday.

The week passed. Every night, she unplugged the reindeer at bedtime. Thursday, it rained all night. She tried not to worry about him. Friday morning, he seemed fine when she spied on him out the window.

That whole week was worse, somehow, than the first

week. Zoe knew it was not her fault that he had decided to sit out in front of her house in a tent for only he knew how long. That was his choice. It was…something he evidently felt he needed to do.

For no reason she could understand.

Yet, as the two-week mark of his campout on her lawn approached, she found she was less and less able to simply ignore him. Less able to tell herself he could leave anytime he wanted and his confining himself to a ten-foot-by-ten-foot square of brown grass, rain or shine, was not her problem.

God help her, she started to get what he was up to.

She started to think how he was sticking it out, putting himself at great inconvenience, getting by in a tent when he could be in a mansion—no, she didn't think he was suffering exactly. All he had to do was make a call and the black limo would arrive, bringing him whatever he'd just realized he couldn't do without.

But it wasn't convenient. It couldn't be easy. To just sit there, out in the open, day in and day out, in a camp chair or inside the tent, with his only moments of privacy when he walked over to the pool house to use the facilities there.

He was doing exactly what she had told him he had no idea how to do. He was fighting. For her. For the baby she carried. For the possibility that she might get past her locked-in idea of him and see him for the man he really was right now.

He wasn't going anywhere. He wasn't forgetting about her. He wasn't moving on to the next banquet in the endless feast that had always been his life. He had no eye out for the next pretty girl.

That broke her heart.

Broke it—and somehow also mended it again.

Saturday night, she stood in the window next to her Christmas tree and watched him for over an hour. She thought how she loved him. She thought how, if not for him, she never would have survived their time in the jungle.

If not for him, she wouldn't have a job she loved. If not for him, there would be no baby coming. If not for him, the richness, the very *rightness* of her life would be infinitely less so.

When she went to bed, she cried in great, gulping sobs. Until her pillow was so wet that she had to get up and change the pillowcase.

And then finally, she slept. Deeply and dreamlessly all through the night.

In the morning, she got up and put on her slippers and her thick, red winter robe and went outside, where Dax was already sitting in his camp chair, drinking his morning coffee.

He watched her approach. "Good morning, Zoe."

"How about breakfast?"

He smiled then, a tired smile that nonetheless made the morning brighter. "I would love breakfast." He got up and he followed her inside.

He stopped when he got past her small square of entryway and gazed thoughtfully at her tree in the window. "I was beginning to wonder if I would ever see that tree from inside."

She turned to him then. She was tearing up a little. "Oh, Dax…"

He set his Starbucks cup on a side table and held out his arms to her.

There was nothing to do but go into them, to sigh in

relief and joy as he wrapped her tightly in his cherishing embrace.

She tucked herself close to him, felt his lips in her hair. "I love you, Dax."

"And I love you." He took her by the shoulders and held her away enough that he could look in her eyes. The white scar he'd taken in the crash back in August gleamed, pale and jagged as a lightning bolt, on his forehead.

She reached up, traced the shape of it, remembering all they had been through. Together.

And he said, "I love you. And I *am* here, Zoe. I'm not going away. I know I was an idiot when you first told me about the baby. I was a fatheaded fool and I let you down. I am so damn sorry. And all I want is a chance to prove to you how much I've learned. How wrong I've been. Dead wrong. Because I really do want to be a family man. With you. I want our baby. I want our life as it has been—and more. I want our life as it can be, you and me, together, in every way."

Her tears brimmed over. "Yes." There. She had said it. The one word. The word that made their future possible. "Yes, Dax. Together. For a lifetime. I want that, too. I'm finally ready for that, too."

Tenderly, he framed her face, brushing gently with his thumbs at the tears on her cheeks. "I've been thinking, while I sat out there on your lawn with those reindeer of yours. Thinking how in Mexico, you had to fight. Thinking how scared you must have been, with me completely out of it, lost in the fever that almost killed me. You were all alone, fighting for my life and yours, too. I think…you changed me then, Zoe. Because of you, I lived. And after that, I was yours. I belong to you, *with* you. And it's all I want, to be right here, where I belong."

She searched his face, found everything she sought there—and more. "I see now that I was wrong to doubt you. But I don't doubt you anymore."

"Will you…?" His voice trailed off. He seemed almost afraid to ask.

She asked, for him. "Will I marry you?" At his nod, she said the important word again. "Yes. Oh, yes. Dax, I want that now. I want to be your wife. I want to be a family. With you. And with our baby."

He kissed her then. The deepest, truest kiss. And then he scooped her high into his arms and carried her back to bed.

They made slow, tender love. And then they got up and cooked breakfast.

And then later, together in the truest way, they went to Sunday dinner at Bravo Ridge.

No one seemed surprised to see Dax. They welcomed him as one of the family.

Aleta hugged him. "Happy holidays, Dax. I'm so pleased you're here."

"So am I, Aleta. I can't tell you how much."

Six-year-old Kira scolded him. "Dax, there you are."

"Hi, Kira."

She braced her small fists on her hips. "Where have you been?"

"Camping," he told her and glanced up to share a grin with Zoe.

Kira reached out and tugged on his hand. "But you're back with our family now?"

"Yes, I am." He gave the child his warmest smile. "I'm back. I promise."

"You'll be with our family for Christmas?" Kira demanded to know.

"Yes," he said. "For Christmas, definitely."

"Good," Kira declared with a nod and then giggled as her grandfather scooped her high in his arms. "Grandpa, you *surprised* me!"

Davis winked at Dax and then lifted the little girl higher still, so she sat on his shoulders. "Let's go eat, Kira."

She linked her arms around his neck and braced her little chin on the top of his silver head. "Okay, Grandpa. Let's go now!" He turned and carried her off toward the kitchen.

Dax held out his hand to Zoe. She took it.

They went in to dinner together, as they were meant to be. For Christmas. In the New Year. And for all the New Years to come.

* * * * *

Watch for Abilene Bravo's story,
DONOVAN'S CHILD,
coming in February 2011,
only from Silhouette Special Edition.

SPECIAL EDITION

COMING NEXT MONTH

Available November 30, 2010

#2083 A THUNDER CANYON CHRISTMAS
RaeAnne Thayne
Montana Mavericks: Thunder Canyon Cowboys

#2084 UNWRAPPING THE PLAYBOY
Marie Ferrarella
Matchmaking Mamas

#2085 THE BACHELOR'S CHRISTMAS BRIDE
Victoria Pade
Northbridge Nuptials

#2086 ONCE UPON A CHRISTMAS EVE
Christine Flynn
The Hunt for Cinderella

#2087 TWINS UNDER HIS TREE
Karen Rose Smith
The Baby Experts

#2088 THE CHRISTMAS PROPOSITION
Cindy Kirk
Rx for Love

REQUEST YOUR FREE BOOKS!

2 FREE NOVELS PLUS 2 FREE GIFTS!

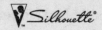

SPECIAL EDITION

Life, Love and Family!

YES! Please send me 2 FREE Silhouette® Special Edition® novels and my 2 FREE gifts (gifts are worth about $10). After receiving them, if I don't wish to receive any more books, I can return the shipping statement marked "cancel." If I don't cancel, I will receive 6 brand-new novels every month and be billed just $4.24 per book in the U.S. or $4.99 per book in Canada. That's a saving of 15% off the cover price! It's quite a bargain! Shipping and handling is just 50¢ per book.* I understand that accepting the 2 free books and gifts places me under no obligation to buy anything. I can always return a shipment and cancel at any time. Even if I never buy another book from Silhouette, the two free books and gifts are mine to keep forever.

235/335 SDN E5RG

Name	(PLEASE PRINT)

Address	Apt. #

City	State/Prov.	Zip/Postal Code

Signature (if under 18, a parent or guardian must sign)

Mail to the **Silhouette Reader Service:**
IN U.S.A.: P.O. Box 1867, Buffalo, NY 14240-1867
IN CANADA: P.O. Box 609, Fort Erie, Ontario L2A 5X3

Not valid for current subscribers to Silhouette Special Edition books.

Want to try two free books from another line?
Call 1-800-873-8635 or visit www.morefreebooks.com.

* Terms and prices subject to change without notice. Prices do not include applicable taxes. N.Y. residents add applicable sales tax. Canadian residents will be charged applicable provincial taxes and GST. Offer not valid in Quebec. This offer is limited to one order per household. All orders subject to approval. Credit or debit balances in a customer's account(s) may be offset by any other outstanding balance owed by or to the customer. Please allow 4 to 6 weeks for delivery. Offer available while quantities last.

Your Privacy: Silhouette is committed to protecting your privacy. Our Privacy Policy is available online at www.eHarlequin.com or upon request from the Reader Service. From time to time we make our lists of customers available to reputable third parties who may have a product or service of interest to you. If you would prefer we not share your name and address, please check here. ☐

Help us get it right—We strive for accurate, respectful and relevant communications. To clarify or modify your communication preferences, visit us at www.ReaderService.com/consumerschoice.

SSE10R

HARLEQUIN®

A *Romance*

FOR EVERY MOOD™

Spotlight on

Classic

Quintessential, modern love stories
that are romance at its finest.

See the next page
to enjoy a sneak peek from
the Harlequin® Romance series.

*See below for a sneak peek from our classic
Harlequin® Romance® line.*

Introducing DADDY BY CHRISTMAS by Patricia Thayer.

MIA caught sight of Jarrett when he walked into the open lobby. It was hard not to notice the man. In a charcoal business suit with a crisp white shirt and striped tie covered by a dark trench coat, he looked more Wall Street than small-town Colorado.

Mia couldn't blame him for keeping his distance. He was probably tired of taking care of her.

Besides, why would a man like Jarrett McKane be interested in her? Why would he want to take on a woman expecting a baby? Yet he'd done so many things for her. He'd been there when she'd needed him most. How could she not care about a man like that?

Heart pounding in her ears, she walked up behind him. Jarrett turned to face her. "Did you get enough sleep last night?"

"Yes, thanks to you," she said, wondering if he'd thought about their kiss. Her gaze went to his mouth, then she quickly glanced away. "And thank you for not bringing up my meltdown."

Jarrett couldn't stop looking at Mia. Blue was definitely her color, bringing out the richness of her eyes.

"What meltdown?" he said, trying hard to focus on what she was saying. "You were just exhausted from lack of sleep and worried about your baby."

He couldn't help remembering how, during the night, he'd kept going in to watch her sleep. How strange was that? "I hope you got enough rest."

She nodded. "Plenty. And you're a good neighbor for

coming to my rescue."

He tensed. Neighbor? *What neighbor kisses you like I did?* "That's me, just the full-service landlord," he said, trying to keep the sarcasm out of his voice. He started to leave, but she put her hand on his arm.

"Jarrett, what I meant was you went beyond helping me." Her eyes searched his face. "I've asked far too much of you."

"Did you hear me complain?"

She shook her head. "You should. I feel like I've taken advantage."

"Like I said, I haven't minded."

"And I'm grateful for everything…"

Grasping her hand on his arm, Jarrett leaned forward. The memory of last night's kiss had him aching for another. "I didn't do it for your gratitude, Mia."

Gorgeous tycoon Jarrett McKane has never believed in Christmas—but he can't help being drawn to soon-to-be-mom Mia Saunders! Christmases past were spent alone…and now Jarrett may just have a fairy-tale ending for all his Christmases future!

Available December 2010, only from Harlequin® Romance®.

HREXP1210

Silhouette® *Desire*

USA TODAY bestselling authors

MAUREEN CHILD

and

SANDRA HYATT

UNDER THE MILLIONAIRE'S MISTLETOE

Just when these leading men thought they had it all figured out, they quickly learn their hearts have made other plans. Two passionate stories about love, longing and the infinite possibilities of kissing under the mistletoe.

Available December wherever you buy books.

Always Powerful, Passionate and Provocative.

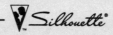

SPECIAL EDITION

USA TODAY BESTSELLING AUTHOR

MARIE FERRARELLA

BRINGS YOU ANOTHER
HEARTWARMING STORY FROM

When Lilli McCall disappeared on him
after he proposed, Kullen Manetti swore
never to fall in love again. Eight years later
Lilli is back in his life, threatening to break
down all the walls he's put up to
safeguard his heart.

UNWRAPPING
THE PLAYBOY

*Available December
wherever books are sold.*
